Blackmail for Beginners

J. T. Berry

This book is a work of fiction. Any references to historical events, real people, or real places are used fictitiously. Other names, characters, places, and events are products of the author's imagination, and any resemblance to actual events or places or persons, living or dead, is entirely coincidental.

ACKNOWLEDGMENTS

I would like to thank my editors Stacey Goitia and Laura Apger for all of their work on and improvements to this book. The cover was designed and created by Patrick Knowles, to whom thanks are also due. Special thanks go to LJB for all of her insights and encouragement. She read every word of every draft and probably knows these characters better than I do.

CHAPTER ONE

The creepy guy across the street from my store was there again this morning, propping up the wall like it would fall down without him, and chain-smoking his way through a pack of Chesterfields. He was dressed the same as before, in a dark double-breasted suit, a black fedora, and Bogart's trench coat. If he wasn't a private investigator, he was certainly trying to look like one. That was one of the most annoying things about living in LA: everybody dressed like they were auditioning for the movie of their own life. He'd been there for three days in a row now and I wished he would just come over and introduce himself instead of hanging around spooking me. Frankly, I could use the company. I hadn't seen a customer for hours.

The clock on the wall ticked around to 4, and the afternoon rain hit its cue as tightly as a Hollywood hoofer. Outside, ambushed by the sudden cloudburst, people huddled under hastily-unfurled umbrellas or ran for cover. Feeling some mixture of exasperated and exhausted, I thought about closing up early. People didn't come into a bookstore in a rainstorm to buy anything. They came in to kill time till the storm had passed, and I was supposedly running a business here, not a library. Not that you could prove it by today's receipts, which would barely buy me a cup of coffee.

The whole day had been a waste of perfectly good lipstick.

My watcher belted his raincoat, turned up his collar, pulled his hat brim down, and huddled tighter to the wall. Traffic snarled, and a chorus of horns sounded as a young couple stopped their maroon convertible in the middle of the street and struggled to raise the top, laughing like newly-minted lovers as they got drenched. A Ford Super Deluxe, said the encyclopedic part of my brain that catalogued make, model and year of every car I saw. A brand-new 1946, as freshly-painted as their romance.

There was a jolt of lighting that filled the room brighter than daylight and a boom of thunder loud enough to rattle the windows. I dropped the book I'd been gluing back together. Of course, it landed glue side down.

"Darn it," I said softly to myself. I plucked the book from the floor and examined the hairs and dust now embedded in the glue, wondering how I was going to get it all off. The glue on the carpet was setting quickly into a hard patch. That would not be coming out.

A perfect footnote to a Monday to forget.

I watched the sidewalk puddles fill up and overflow into the gutters. Rent was due in a week, and I didn't know how many more days like today I could take, either financially or emotionally. As I inevitably did in low moments, I wondered what was wrong with me. Owning a bookstore ought to be my dream job. I loved books, I loved reading, and I loved that people with used books to sell brought me reads I would never have discovered for myself. It should have been perfect, other than the little matter of barely making enough money to buy food.

But what other prospects were there for a twenty-four year-old woman with an unfinished college degree in German and a bitter distaste for housewifery?

I told myself I definitely wasn't going to get anything more done today. Instead, I was going to treat myself to a cup of coffee I didn't deserve and a slice of cake I couldn't afford. I latched the door and turned the sign to 'Closed'.

I cleaned and put away the glasses I wore only in front of customers, freshened up the perfume behind my ears, and checked myself over in the mirror. I was wearing a thoroughly sensible knee-length gray wool skirt, gently creased in the lap from sitting most of the day; an almost-matching cardigan; a pale blue cotton blouse; and my favorite scarf, an art nouveau print. Head to toe, I looked the very image of this season's impoverished yet smartly-dressed bookseller. If Hollywood were casting the part, they couldn't have done better.

I let down my hair from the tight bun I'd been wearing all day. I fluffed it out, and was rearranging it into a loose ponytail when I heard banging on the door. I stuck my head out of the office to see.

"Closed!" I shouted to the girl outside, pointing to the sign. But the banging continued. I went over and stood right behind the door, pointed down at the sign, and folded my arms.

She folded hers too and yelled through the glass, "Not leaving!"

I gave up. I was supposed to be open until five anyway, and maybe it was an emergency. Maybe somebody desperately needed a lightly-used romance paperback and it absolutely couldn't wait till morning. And maybe I needed the quarter on an afternoon when I hadn't sold anything else. One hour closed was two percent of my opportunity for the week, I calculated. Which was two percent more than I could afford.

Opening the door, I let her slip inside and latched it again behind her. She was wearing sturdy-looking pale khaki-colored gabardine slacks darkened around the cuffs by the rain splashing up from the sidewalk, and a leather flight jacket over a simple, white blouse. On top of her enviably auburn curls, she wore a cap with a number on it in metal characters. Conductor on a streetcar, I guessed. She was about five-five, a couple of inches shorter than my five-seven, and my patent leather heels gave me another inch over her flats. Slim and pretty, she still carried an air of toughness. She wouldn't get into the Marmont dressed like that, but on her, it looked good.

I switched my brain into Professional mode, putting on my most professional voice and best smile. "I was just closing, but if you're looking for something specific, perhaps I can help."

"You… uh… know much about old books?"

I made a show of an exaggerated look around at the shelves. Almost everything I had was old, but not in the good way. The wall to my left displayed Fiction. Crude wooden shelves clumsily coated in once-white, now-yellowing paint went all the way to the ceiling. Section dividers identified Romance, Horror, Crime, Westerns, and something called "Classics," which was mostly Dickens, Austen, and the Brontë sisters.

On my right was Non-Fiction, the shelves here more widely separated to accommodate larger formats. There were sections for history, travel, and biographies, among others.

Within each section, books were arranged mostly alphabetically by author, depending on how diligently customers had put back the books they had browsed. Reshelving them in their correct places was the one task I still reliably enjoyed, although I had learned long ago that it was rude to follow customers around correcting their misfiles while they watched. On rare busy days, I might have to sit twitchily for an hour or more, waiting for an opportunity to put things right.

"You could try me," I eventually said.

"Do you know anything about an 1865 Vanity Fair? First American edition?" she asked, more than a little weariness in her voice. I obviously wasn't the first person she'd tried.

It was a very odd request. Nobody who knew anything about books came to my store for that kind of thing. They went to Hooke's across the street. Mind you, it was hard to say when he might be open, what with him being dead. Hooke's was—or rather, had been until recently—a much nicer bookstore than mine, with gold lettering on the windows promising 'rare and fine books for the discerning collector'. Prestigious items had lain open on easels in the display windows and shelves of leatherbound volumes had filled the interior, many in imposing gold-embossed matching sets. I'd been in just once to check it out, and it was much as I imagined the study of a newly-wealthy Victorian industrialist. Books bought by the foot for decor, not for reading.

And in the back room, known only to a select clientele, Hooke had been running the lending library of fine-art pornography that had gotten him murdered not so long ago.

Now Hooke's was just an empty storefront. The display windows were bare and the glass that protected them was grimy on the outside and dusty on the inside. The store had been unoccupied for three months. The tabloids had been all over the murder with the salacious circumstances and speculation about the still-unknown killer. It was hard to lease a location after so much lewd publicity.

Pulling back from my reverie, I gestured at the fiction shelves and raised an eyebrow. "Does it look like I sell rare first editions?"

"Does it look like I buy rare first editions?" she replied with equal sarcasm, gesturing at her outfit. We stared each other down for a few seconds.

"Okay, so what are you really asking?" I said.

"I'm just after some information. Sorry, I didn't know today was an early closing."

I actually couldn't tell whether or not she was being sarcastic that time. I grudgingly allowed myself to admire her a touch. "Information about what?"

"Did you ever meet a guy called Dalton?"

I gave it some thought. Not about whether I remembered him; I definitely did. But about how I wanted to reply. "Oddly enough, yes. He came by the store about three months ago."

"And what did you talk about?" she prompted.

"He claimed he was a private detective working a case—I think that was supposed to impress me—and flashed a license of some kind. I didn't get a good look, but I probably wouldn't know a real one from a fake even if I did, so I took him at his word. He said he was investigating Hooke and he needed help locating a rare book. He wanted an 1865 Vanity Fair. Same as you, coincidentally. He didn't want to ask about it at Hooke's because it would tip him off to something, but he wouldn't say what exactly. I suggested a couple of other dealers, told him how much he should pay, and that was it. He left and I never saw nor heard from him again."

"And was this around the same time Hooke got bumped off?"

"It was literally the day before. The next day, the murder was all over the evening papers, and then over the next few days, all the prurient details came out. That's why it stuck with me. I never did figure out what the book had to do with the case, if anything. Did I get Hooke killed?"

"Probably not. Listen, I need to talk to you. Can I buy you a drink?"

Why not? I thought. I could do with a free coffee. And I obviously wasn't doing anything more worthwhile.

We didn't go for coffee. Instead, we walked a couple of blocks west to a bar she knew. The rain had lightened up and we didn't need my umbrella. She had introduced herself as Joy D'Amico, and I told her to call me Dot because I had always hated the name Dorothy. It had only gotten worse since The Wizard of Oz came out a few years back, and everybody thought they were the first person to tell me to click my heels together. When she asked me if my boss would be okay with me closing early, I let it drop that I owned the place.

We walked the rest of the way in silence while she chewed on that.

The daylight was starting to go and lights were on in the storefronts. The pavement was as black as a river and reflections like a broken kaleidoscope twinkled up at us from the oily puddles in the street. I was reminded once again how much of a divide the middle of the boulevard represented. On my side of the street, the south, there were low clapboard buildings with utilitarian businesses: a hardware store, a laundromat, a radio repair shop, and apparently, a bar I had never paid any attention to. The north side faced us down with two-story brick frontages hosting, besides Hooke's, a fine art gallery, a parfumerie, a men's bespoke tailor, an antique store of the kind where prices are not marked, and a jeweler where the prices depend on whether you're buying for your wife, your mistress, or your wife who had found out about your mistress.

The bar was pretty dark inside and I couldn't see much at first, but the smell of stale beer and cheap floor cleaner told me right away what sort of place we were in. The furniture was heavy and coarse and had absorbed years of damp and alcohol fumes, and now seemed to also absorb whatever light filtered in. It was fairly small, with no more than a dozen tables and a couple of booths against one wall. It was the sort of place I assumed working men came to drink and hopes came to die.

As soon as the door closed behind us, a handful of men at a table in back called out to Joy, and she hailed them back. By the time my eyes adjusted to the dark, the bartender had already pulled a beer for Joy and was leaning forward on the bar, looking at me impatiently, as if he had a crowd of people waiting to be served. He didn't. He wasn't particularly tall, but he was hefty and had a face you didn't want to argue with. I guessed keeping bar in such a down-at-heel place attracted the kind of men who could shut down trouble before it started, rather than deal with it after.

"Shoot," Joy said to me. "I'm guessing you're not really much of a beer drinker. This isn't exactly a cocktails and linen napkins kind of place."

"Don't worry," I replied. "I'm sure they have something I'll drink." I turned to the barman. "Rye. Neat. Two fingers."

He reached for the bottle in the well, saw the look on my face, and went up a couple of shelves for the good stuff.

"My tab, Jack," Joy told the barman.

We pulled a couple of stools up to a high top and hoisted ourselves inelegantly onto them. I sipped a little rye and we got our cigarettes started—Kool for me and Lucky Strike for her.

"Rye drinker, huh?" said Joy, probably just for something to say.

"It was the first thing I learned to drink," I explained. "When I turned twenty-one, my father poured a shot each of brandy, rye, and gin, and told me to pick one. I liked the rye best, and I've stuck with it ever since. I've been told it's no drink for a lady, so I guess I'm no lady."

"Listen, I should say sorry for earlier, thinking you were just a shopgirl."

"That's okay, and this makes us straight," I said, picking up the rye and tapping it against her beer glass. "You have no idea how often people tell me they want to talk to the owner. If I'm feeling especially annoyed at them, I'll tell them to wait, go into the office, rearrange my hair, come back out again, and as sweetly as I can, ask how I can help. It might not be good for business, but it's good for the soul."

She laughed. I thought maybe I didn't completely dislike her after all. Or maybe it was the rye.

That seemed like enough small talk for Joy, which was more than fine with me, and she jumped right into the reason we were there. "About Dalton. The thing is, he's missing. He stood me up a week ago and I haven't heard from him since."

I arched my eyebrows. "Being stood up for a date doesn't seem like it's worth this kind of drama."

"Woah, back up! I'm not dating him, no. Working for him. Driving. I'm a cabbie."

She pointed at the cap she'd set on the table when we sat down. Now the shoes made sense, too. I wouldn't want to drive in heels all day either.

"Oh. Now I owe you an apology. I assumed you were a streetcar conductor or something. Not many women are driving cabs these days, now the men are back."

"You're right about that last part. Every day I come to work, I worry they're going to tell me they gave my shift to a vet and I don't get to drive anymore. Driving for Dalton was insurance in a way. I've been doing jobs for him a handful of times a week, ever since I met him during the Hooke business. Sometimes he'd hire me more, depending on what he was working. Tail jobs on cheating husbands or insurance fraudsters, deliveries and pick-ups, or just generally running him around. All kinds of stuff, really. Anyway, last Monday, I was supposed to pick him up outside his building, but he never showed. I waited half an hour before I gave up. He's never been even five minutes late before. The next couple of days, I called his office a few times, but nobody picked up. I left messages with his service, too, but never got a call back."

I raised my eyebrows again and took a more thoughtful sip of rye.

"There's nobody else you could try? Friends of his?"

"He never talked about any friends," she said. "He once mentioned he was dating some classy society dame with oil money, but I don't know her name. He kept his personal life pretty much to himself."

"I'll admit that does sound like a bigger deal than a missed date. But does it have to mean that something bad happened? Maybe his rich lady friend persuaded him that he didn't have to creep around sleazy hotels, following cheating husbands to scrape a living, and they retired to Palm Springs to be idle and rich together."

"Nah, that sounds pretty cock-eyed to me. Uh, no offense. I mean, I don't see Dalton as the easily-retired type. Besides, he would at least have called to say goodbye, right?"

She crushed the butt of her cigarette in the ashtray, pulled out another, and I lit it for her with my Zippo. "A nice guy certainly would. Maybe Dalton just isn't as nice a guy as you thought. Or maybe Miss Rich and Classy told him to knock it off with the calls to the pretty cabbie lady," I said.

Joy blushed faintly at the compliment.

"Anyway," I continued, "why don't you take this to the police? Sounds like a job for Missing Persons."

"You mean like this?" she said. She put on her cap, sat up straight, and mimed picking up a telephone. Lowering her voice as far as it would go, she said, "Police station, how can I help? You say a six foot tall, well-built private detective who can handle himself in a fight isn't returning your calls, Miss? Would you like to date one of our detectives instead?" She mimed hanging up, took off her cap, and resumed her slouch.

I scowled, embarrassed. "Fair enough. But what do you imagine I can do?"

"I don't know, but I'm all out of ideas. You're the only other person I've found who knows Dalton, even a little bit."

"How did you even find me?"

"He told me about a bookseller who helped with the Vanity Fair. So I've spent the day dropping into used bookstores between fares, asking about it to see who bites. Mostly collecting funny looks and weak passes. If I was smarter, I would have started with the store right across the street from Hooke's place."

"Okay, but still. What's this to me?"

"Listen, you don't know what type of people he mixes it with. By the time the Hooke business was all wrapped, there were three men dead, and Dalton could easily have been number four, the way he told it. I don't know if this is blowback from that case or something else completely, but he takes risks, and maybe he took one too many."

I shrugged. "I agree it sounds bad, and I wish I had a lead for you. But I met him one time and I'm very sure I don't know anything you don't already know. Truly. Thanks for the drink, but I have to go now." I stubbed out my cigarette, got up from the table, told her good luck, and meant it.

"Wait," she said, and pulled a business card out of her jacket's inside pocket. It had a number for Red Star Taxis. "If you think of anything, call me, okay? The dispatcher will take a message and it'll find me."

I walked home to my dark and under-furnished bachelor apartment, made a simple dinner, listened to the radio, and tried to forget about Dalton, Hooke, and my part in it all. I fell asleep thinking I'd heard the last of the business.

Chapter Two

Tuesday morning was bright and sharp with the inevitable rain forecast for the late afternoon. A weatherman could make a good living in LA predicting 'same as yesterday'. I'd picked out a plain navy blue cotton dress I regularly wore to the shop, unflattering but low-maintenance, and my raincoat. Most of what I laughingly called my wardrobe was some shade of blue or gray; it saved a lot of thinking about what to wear, and let me easily mix the few decent items I could afford to own. I reflected, not for the first time, that nothing in my wardrobe was suitable for LA's winters. I was invariably too cold in the mornings, too hot in the afternoons, and too sweaty in the after-rain humidity. I wondered why anybody chose to live in this kooky town.

I was half a block from the store when I noticed a huddle of people around my storefront. I didn't think it was my window display attracting the sidewalk crowd, and I quickened my step. As I got close, I saw a patrolman barring the door. He was not much taller than me, heavily built and soft around the middle. The kind word would be 'stout'. Maybe around fifty years old. If so, probably close to a full pension retirement, and happy to be working easy assignments like crowd control outside a bookstore. The uniform would probably be the last he'd have to buy, even though it was shiny at the knees and elbows. I started to wonder what retired cops did for second careers, but stopped myself. I didn't have time for idle speculation right now.

I introduced myself, showed him my door key, and he told me what was going on.

"There was a break-in sometime last night. The place is a mess and we don't know what was taken. We don't get a lot of used book thieves around here."

It seemed to me there was an unpleasant sneer to the way he said that. "Any ideas who did it?" I asked.

"Who knows? Maybe a wino looking for a place to drink and sleep it off without getting rousted. Or just a bum after the contents of the till. I don't expect there was anything else worth taking."

The sneer was definitely there. He didn't strike me as the sort of cop who placed a lot of value on reading.

"What happens now? Will a detective take a look at the scene?"

"Oh, sure. Major crime like this, they'll probably form a task force. Put out an alert and call for witnesses."

I gave him my best glare. He'd seen better. He handed me a form with some scribbled writing, most of it inside the boxes. The printed parts were legible. "Here's your police report. You'll need it for your insurance claim. And if I were you, I'd add a few valuables to what you lost, if you know what I mean."

And with that, he ambled away, leaving the crowd to disperse in its own time. Case closed.

I opened the door and cautiously stepped inside, glass crunching under my pumps. It looked like the burglar had knocked in one pane of glass in the door and simply reached inside to unlatch it. The break-in was neat and tidy, but the rest of the place was a mess. The display table had been turned over, its contents spilled on the floor. The drawers of the desk that served as my counter had been pulled out, emptied, and the bottoms smashed. Nothing on the shelves had been touched, thankfully. Surprisingly, what little money I left in the till overnight was still there. I went through to my back office. It had been completely tossed. Books, catalogs, paperwork everywhere. Every shelf cleared, here too the drawers emptied and broken. The disorder was viscerally distressing. For several seconds, I felt like I might throw up or pass out.

I returned to the front of the store and slumped in my chair. That was when I noticed the note on my desk. In large, blocky capitals it said:

GIVE IT UP

I stared at it for a minute. It meant absolutely nothing to me. Give what up?

Reluctantly, I returned my attention to the disaster spread around me. I had a lot of things I needed to do. I ought to start tidying up. Take inventory of what was missing or damaged. File an insurance claim. Remember I hadn't been able to afford to renew my insurance. Get the door repaired. Get the store back up and running as soon as possible if I wanted to eat as well as pay my rent.

I didn't do any of those things. Instead I opened my purse, pulled out Joy's card, and dialed Red Star Taxis. The dispatcher took my message. I stared at my shaking hands as though they belonged to somebody else, clumsily lit a cigarette, and waited.

Chapter Three

Sat amongst the mess of my office, I tried to take my cigarette slowly as I waited for a callback from Joy. The dispatcher called me back about fifteen minutes later and told me to wait for Joy at Jack's bar. I walked over and was surprised to discover it was open, even though it was barely 9 a.m. A neon sign in the window said 'We Never Close', and I was almost ready to believe it. I decided that a drink might help with my nerves.

By the time Joy got to the bar, I was starting on my second shot of rye. I'd also clumsily lit and chain-smoked two menthols, and my hands were still trembling visibly. I'd struggled to get the first few sips of rye down without spilling any, eventually wrapping the shot glass in my handkerchief so as not to splash anything on the table. Which was ridiculous; these tables had obviously seen far worse than anything I could do with a few drops of rye.

There was an implicit threat in the note that had me more worried than any explicit threat might have done. My body was urging me towards fight of flight, and I couldn't do either. It was shredding my nerves.

I had the bar to myself until Joy arrived. She saw I had a rye in front of me and ordered a beer to keep me company.

"My tab," I told the barman, a different guy from yesterday, in imitation of Joy's call the previous day. Apparently, Jack didn't work the day shift.

I waited for Joy to settle herself. She took a draw of her beer, pulled out one of her Luckies and lit it, and asked if I was okay. I showed her my trembling hands but told her I was getting there. The rye and the cigarettes were kicking in, finally.

"Dispatch got your message to me. I came as soon as I could get off. Did they take anything valuable?" said Joy.

I snorted. "I don't have anything valuable. It's 'Stone's Used Books', not 'Hooke's Antiquarian Books and Collectors' Editions'. I have a few decent hardcovers, but it's mostly cheap paperbacks that I can turn over quickly and make a nickel on."

"What were they after, then?"

"The patrol cop said it was probably just random, a drunk looking for a place to sleep, or a burglar looking for an easy score. But that makes no sense."

"Why not?"

"Look at the details. The table was turned over, but none of the hardbacks were taken. And that would have been noisy, and risk attracting attention, so why do it? And why make such a mess? That doesn't sound like a burglar, nor somebody looking for a crib for the night. And on top of all that, there's the note, which apparently the cop completely missed."

"They left a note?"

"Yes. It said 'give it up'. Whatever 'it' is."

Joy took another drag of her beer and her cigarette in quick succession. She tapped her ash onto the floor, ignoring the ashtray I'd been steadily filling. "The cop probably didn't even go inside. Just stuck his head in the door, saw it was a break-in, and decided that was enough work for the morning. So, now what?"

"I suppose I should show the note to the police."

"Hah! They're not going to do anything with a note like that. They'll just tell you they're working on it, then drop it in the round file as soon as your back is turned. They might not even wait that long."

"What then? I sit around waiting for somebody to come back and threaten me for something I don't have? That sounds like a recipe for sleepless nights and anxious days."

"Yeah, and I don't think they're going to take 'sorry, I don't have it' for an answer."

We both stared into drinks and let our cigarettes burn down.

"I wish Dalton was here right now," said Joy eventually.

"Sorry, but I think we're on our own with this," I replied. "If we had some idea what on Earth they want, it would help."

"Sure, but how are we going to figure that out?"

"Let's take it logically." Logic was always firm ground for me. "The note obviously means the break-in was purposeful, not random."

"So what are you hiding in there?"

"Nothing. Like I said, I don't have any valuables. I don't have any secrets. I don't even have a safe. There's nothing remotely interesting about me. I go to work, I buy and sell used books, I go home. Whatever they are thinking I have, I definitely don't have it."

"What does that leave?"

"It leaves the only interesting thing about me: you. It can't be a coincidence that you came to ask me about a book I obviously don't sell, in search of a detective missing after a dangerous case, and that very night my store is broken into. But how are they connected? And why is that reason enough to break in and smash up my store?"

"Is the book valuable?"

"A first American edition of Vanity Fair? It's not cheap if it's in good condition, maybe a few hundred dollars. Obviously not as much as the first British edition, but certainly a whole lot more than anything in my store. If that's what they were after it would explain why they didn't bother with the paperbacks on the shelves. But like I said, I can't imagine why anybody would think I have one. And it's not exactly impossible to just buy one somewhere else if you want one that badly. If they'd asked politely I would have sent them to the same places I sent Dalton."

I took a pause to light another cigarette from the stub of the one I was finishing. Chain smoking wasn't a great habit, not least because it could get expensive, but I gave myself a pass given the morning I'd had.

"The detail that's bothering me is why they smashed the drawers," I continued. "How does that fit?"

"False bottoms?" said Joy. Seeing my quizzical eyebrow, she explained. "Sometimes drawers have a false bottom to hide valuables. It happens all the time in detective stories."

I must have looked amused.

"Hey, so I read a lot of cheap detective novels," she added, defensively.

"I'm not judging. I sell a lot of cheap detective novels," I replied. "But in that case, definitely not looking for the Vanity Fair. A compartment large enough to hold it would be really obvious just by looking at the drawers. The book is over 600 pages long."

Joy waved to the barman for another beer. It was the first time I'd seen a woman drink two beers before lunch. Mind you, I'd drunk two shots of rye so I probably shouldn't judge her for that either.

"If we rule out the Vanity Fair, then what? You still think it's connected to Dalton being missing?"

"I'm convinced of it. Nothing else makes sense, apart from total coincidence. And I don't like coincidence."

I took another sip of rye, stared off into the distance, and contemplated everything we'd put together so far. "Let's suppose somebody wants something Dalton has. Not the book, but perhaps something he came across while investigating a case"

"Right. Something valuable to them. Or maybe evidence dangerous to them."

"Something like that. Either way, Dalton is nowhere to be found, so they suspect maybe he gave it to you for safekeeping. Or at least, you might know where he hid it. They follow you around for a while hoping you might tip them off to the location. Then they see you go to my shop, and see us leave together and go for a friendly drink. Bingo, you must have stashed it with me. Whatever it is."

"Okay, that's a good story. It kind of makes me think of The Man Who Knew Too Much, or maybe The Thirty Nine Steps."

I must have looked puzzled again.

"Hitchcock movies," she explained. "He loves set-ups where the bad guys think an ordinary Joe knows something he doesn't, and they're chasing him for it while he tries to figure out what it is they're after. And I've had a feeling somebody might be following me. I keep seeing a green Packard hanging half a block back, just the way I would do it."

"There's been a guy watching my store for the past few days too."

"Even before I came to see you?" said Joy, her eyebrows raised.

"Good point," I replied. "Maybe they already connected me to Dalton before you showed up."

We both sipped our drinks in silence for a few moments. My nerves had somewhat settled now. We were no closer to figuring this out, but simply reasoning about it helped me.

The silence was interrupted by Joy. "I just had a bad thought," she said, worry etched in her frown.

"What?" I asked.

"If Dalton went into hiding, surely he'd realize they'd come after me. And I don't think he'd leave me hanging in the wind like this without so much as a heads-up. That doesn't seem like him at all."

"I'll have to take your word for that. But if so, then where is he?"

"I hate to say this out loud, but maybe somebody has snatched him. Suppose he doesn't have it on him, and won't give it up. When he doesn't talk, they decide to come after me."

"And now me."

"So now what happens?" Joy asked.

"What would you do if you were them?"

"If I were in a Hitchcock movie, I'd come after us again, to see if we know anything. That note for sure sounds like they'll be back."

That made me anxious all over again, but I resisted the urge to order a third shot.

"And I don't know if they'll believe us when we say we don't. The note sounds like they're not in any doubt." I replied miserably.

"Call me crazy, but I'm thinking we need to get ahead of this thing before something worse happens."

"Yes," I agreed. "Take this into our own hands. Try to find the whatever-it-is." It might not be smart, but it was ruthlessly logical.

"Okay then, let's run with this. Any thoughts about what we're looking for?" asked Joy.

"Good question. It has to be something bigger than a sheet of paper but small enough to fit in your secret compartment."

"How do you figure it's not just a sheet of paper?"

"Because they wouldn't bother searching a bookstore for one sheet of paper. It could be in a million places, between two books, even between the pages of a book. They'd never find it unless they knew exactly what book to look in, maybe even which page."

"Okay, yeah, that tracks. But that still leaves a mountain of possibilities. And where we would even start looking?"

I considered that. "I can only think of one place to start. You know where his office is, right? We should search it. Even if the whatever-it-is isn't there, it might tell us something." It sounded like a long shot, yet still better than any alternative.

"I went by his office on Friday. It was locked."

"Leave that to me," I told her.

"I hope you're not thinking of breaking in," said Joy, uncertainly.

"Don't worry, I know a trick or two", I promised her.

She stared into her beer in case it had any secret wisdom to share, than looked me in the eye. "Are we crazy? I feel like we might be crazy."

"We might be, but I can't just wait around for whoever wrecked my store to show up again, and hope they accept a polite No."

I finished my rye and told Joy I had to get back to the store and see about cleaning up, and maybe even selling some books.

"As long as you're okay," she said. "I've got a shift to finish".

We agreed to meet the next morning at eight in front of my store.

When I got back to the shop, the door was closed, the window pane repaired. The putty was still soft to the touch. Inside, I found a note on my desk from George, the elderly man who ran the hardware store two doors up, explaining he had fixed the glass without waiting to be asked because he saw it needed doing. He hadn't left a bill because he knew I couldn't afford to pay him.

He'd also stood the table back up and stacked the books on it. Of course, he put them in the wrong places and none of the stacks were square, but still, it was thoughtful. The note said not to open and close the door too much until the putty had dried, so I propped it open with a hefty Latin dictionary I'd bought thinking I might teach myself the language in my down time. Tidying the office was too much for me right then; better to leave it for after closing.

Business was brisk for once and I spent most of the day with my professional face on. Some of it, unsurprisingly, was sightseers who had heard about the break-in. It was probably the most exciting thing on our block since the Hooke murder. One young couple nuzzled their way around the entire fiction section before finally buying each other gifts, an Agatha Christie for her and a Sherlock Holmes for him.

A couple in their fifties paged through a large-format photographic guide to Paris together, laughing and smiling and reminiscing about their long-ago trip. I fully expected them to put it back when they were done, but they surprised me. It was by some margin my best sale in many days. A man in his late teens or early twenties in chinos and a tab collar shirt - college student, perhaps? - brought in a brand new matching set of the six most popular Dickens novels, undoubtedly an unwanted Christmas present. Those would be an easy resale and a nice profit. He even accepted store credit in payment, so a double win. Store credit was my best-selling item, and my most profitable, too, especially when people didn't come back to use it.

A gaggle of men with military haircuts and civilian clothes, recently demobilized I guessed, came in and bought a dozen westerns which, they told me, they would pass around between them until they fell apart, and, they promised, afterwards they would come back for more.

By the time I closed at five pm, I was exhausted. I was physically fatigued from being on my feet and mentally drained from faking professionalism. Selling is tough on someone who doesn't like people very much. On the other hand, I had done more business today than I had in a long time. And the shop was a lot more tolerable when it was busy. Or to be precise, when I was busy. Left to itself, my mood would sink under gravity. A few good sales and a couple of interesting questions from prospective customers were what it took to lift it again.

If the week continued like this, I might still make rent, I thought. And maybe even have something left over for food. Surely I deserved at least a little celebration. My usual choice was a tea room a couple of blocks away for coffee and a cake, but today felt different. Maybe if I walked over to Jack's bar I might catch Joy coming off shift. I was starting to like talking to her.

On the way over, I tried to wrestle my feelings about the store to the ground. On the one hand I felt happy, almost elated, at the day's business. On the other hand, I hated being an imposter all day. And I still wasn't looking forward to the following day with anything like pleasant anticipation. The job would be a lot more fun if I didn't have to deal with customers. My arrival at the bar ended my tail-chasing thoughts.

When I stepped inside, Jack himself was back behind the counter. Jack must work the evening and night shift, I thought, and possibly even owned the joint. Apparently, he recognized me because he held up a shot glass, and when I gave him the thumbs-up, he reached up for the good rye and my drink was poured by the time I reached him.

"Tab?" Jack asked.

"Sure," I replied. I assumed he was asking if I wanted one, not whose to put it on. I didn't have a lot of experience with this kind of thing.

Turning away from the counter, I immediately spotted a clutch of drivers around a rectangular table over in the far corner, and from the back, Joy's unmistakable auburn curls. One of the drivers waved to me and Joy turned around to see what was happening. Seeing me, she immediately scraped her chair back and got up, meeting me halfway across the room.

"Can we get a table and have a drink together?" I asked. "I'm celebrating a good day at the store offsetting this morning's disaster."

"Better idea", replied Joy. "You come and have a drink with all of us!"

My first thought was a firm 'no'. I hated large groups. I hated meeting strangers. I hated making polite small talk. Worst of all, I knew there would be several conversations going on crossing each other, and my brain would try to follow all of them and end up catching none of them. After a day of faking it with customers, the last thing I needed was more pretending with Joy's friends.

My treacherous mouth said 'yes'.

There was a general shuffling of chairs and a space opened up between Joy and an older lady. One of the drivers filled it with a chair from another table and I sat down.

"This is Dot, my partner in crime!"

Apparently, Joy had told them what we were planning for the next day.

"She owns a bookstore, and she's very smart," continued Joy. "So you all be respectful or she'll put you down in ways you won't even understand." That got a laugh. Then Joy had them go around the table and say their names for me. I immediately forgot all of them except the woman on my right was Madge. She was the dispatcher I had spoken to earlier. She was a short, rotund woman in her late fifties, I guessed, with gray hair dyed blue and permed. It quickly became clear she was den mother to the troop, reigning in the banter when it veered too close to what she considered unsuitable for my ears, quieting down any squabbles getting out of hand, and generally keeping eight grown men in order without ever appearing to be in charge.

I tried to limit my conversation to Joy and Madge and whoever joined in with us, and shut out the other conversations at the table. Before I knew it, a couple of hours and three shots of rye had gone by and I'd had a much better time than I ever could have anticipated. Somewhere along the way, I had dropped my mask and just become myself. But now that I was watching myself again, I could feel my anxiety rising and the cacophony of other voices starting to intrude and demand my attention. I abruptly rose from my chair and said a general goodbye to the table.

Joy jumped up to join me and walked with me to the bar where I settled my tab. For a moment, I was terrified she was going to try to hug me. Instead, we simply reaffirmed our plan for the morning and I caught a streetcar home, worrying quietly about the amount of rye I'd consumed that day.

Chapter Four

A few minutes after eight the next morning, Joy pulled her cab up in front of my store. I was already outside waiting for her. Her taxi today was a 1939 DeSoto De Luxe long wheelbase, a popular model with cab companies, the year readily identifiable from the distinctive oval headlights. We found a parking spot a block away from the building where Dalton rented an office and walked the rest. It was an averagely perfect LA morning, bright, sunny, cloudless, comfortably warm for the time of year.

Today's outfit was the closest thing I owned to a suit, a sky-blue skirt that ended just above the knee and had just enough movement for dancing, which was something I never did and desperately missed these days; a matching bolero jacket; and a white cotton blouse that buttoned all the way up to my throat. I matched it with black pumps and wore my raincoat over the top for the inevitable rain later. I'd washed and dried my one good pair of nylons and was wearing them again. Joy was wearing what I was coming to think of as her driver's uniform of gabardine slacks, white blouse, and pilot's jacket.

Dalton's office was in an unremarkable brick building, five stories, stone caps and sills around the windows in a forlorn attempt to add some class. If you didn't have the number you would never pick it out from the rest of the block, and I was glad Joy had been there before. All the woodwork was a couple of years overdue for painting, but the same was true of a lot of the buildings around the neighborhood. Maybe now the war was over there would be somebody to do it, and paint to do it with.

We walked up the steps together and pushed through the double doors side by side like we belonged there. The lobby was every bit as shabby as the exterior. Everything painted needed repainting, and everything metal needed polishing. The elevator operator was a tired and stooped Mexican man with cropped white hair and mahogany skin who looked to be somewhere between sixty and a hundred years old. He nodded to Joy's request for the third floor and took us up without saying a word or looking at us. He opened the concertina gate, pointed us down a threadbare carpet towards Dalton's office, closed the gate behind us, and disappeared into the floor.

We found the door, wood with a single pane of frosted glass, no light inside, and the words "J. Dalton, Private Investigator" painted in white letters with a gold outline on the glass. Joy listened cautiously at the door for a moment and tried the handle. "Like I said, locked," she muttered, rattling it to underscore her point. "Now what?"

"I've got this," I told her. I pulled a couple of bobby pins from my hair, and straightened them out. Kneeling down, I began to work on the lock. "It's a basic Yale lock, not too difficult. The art is not leaving any marks to show you picked it," I told her as I fiddled. "Ah!" I exclaimed as I felt the last pin shift.

"Where did you learn that?" Joy asked.

"From a book, would you believe? It's the first time I ever got to use it for real, though. I wasn't even sure it would work, which would have been embarrassing." I was starting to feel an inkling of excitement about our adventure.

"Well, it's still entering, but not breaking, I guess."

I turned the handle and tentatively pushed the door open. I groped the wall until I found the light switch and we stepped into the outer office, set up as a waiting room. It was small and windowless, the walls painted the same soothing shade of teal you find in prisons, high schools, and sanitariums, and probably for the same reason. There was a two-seater couch with slightly ragged upholstery against the opposite wall, next to the solid wood door to the inner office; a faded print of a nondescript landscape above the couch; and a small coffee table in front of it. A few well-thumbed magazines were scattered across the table, and in front of it lay the supine body of a dead man.

The carpet was dull brown in color except for the dark black patch of dried blood around the man's head. He looked to be about medium height, though it was hard to be sure with him lying down, and wearing a cheap brown suit and nearly-matching loafers. A bright purple display handkerchief poked incongruously from his top pocket. No hat to be seen. His hair was completely white, almost transparent. A part of my brain was demanding I worry about how that blood stain would come out.

Joy reacted first; she closed and locked the door behind us, and we both stared in silence.

It didn't take a doctor to see he was gone. His hands were bluish-purple and his face was tinged with green. His eyelids were half open, and a grayish haze covered his eyes like nothing I had ever seen on a living person. There were no obvious wounds to his front, and I guessed he had been struck on the back of the head.

"You should check his pockets," I told Joy, surprised at how level my own voice sounded.

"You check them!" she exclaimed. "I ain't touching the stiff!"

We both stood contemplating the body for another minute. "Maybe we shouldn't touch it at all, and leave it for the police," I finally said.

Joy nodded her agreement. I stepped over his legs and tried the door to the inner office. To my surprise, it was unlocked. I found the light switch and turned it on.

"What are you doing?" asked Joy. "There's a dead body here! We have to leave before cops show up."

I turned to her, my hand still on the door handle. "The cops aren't coming," I said as steadily as I could manage, although I felt a slight tremor in my voice now. "He's been dead for hours for the blood to have dried like that. If they knew, they'd have been here long ago. And the elevator man obviously doesn't come by, so we can take our time."

Joy sighed. "Alright. But let's be careful." She turned off the light in the waiting room and followed me into the inner office to close the door behind us. "Now at least nobody else is going to try to come in."

The inner office was as unremarkable as the outer one. A heavy, wooden desk, a worn scuffed leather swivel chair behind it, two uncomfortable-looking wooden chairs in front, all of it well-used. On top of the desk sat a blotter, an empty inkwell without a pen, a week-per-page diary open to a couple of weeks ago, a phone, two ashtrays, and a box of

Kleenex set near the front edge. I guessed you got a lot of criers in the detective business. Apart from the Kleenex, it could have been the desk of an insurance salesman. The dust on top said the office hadn't been cleaned in a couple of weeks. Against the far wall was a row of three metal file cabinets, three drawers each, the kind you would see in any office.

I sat in the swivel chair and turned rhythmically back and forth. I flicked backwards and forwards a few pages in the diary; I suppose I was hoping some dramatic note in block capitals with exclamation marks and circled three times would leap out at me, but every page looked like the others, just a few scattered names and notes. The desk had two drawers to my left and I pulled open the top one. There was a phone book and a mostly-full half-pint bottle of rye. As soon as I saw it I knew I needed a shot; the fact of a dead body just outside the door was starting to register with me. I took a slug, screwed the top on tight, and dropped it in my purse. I suspected I might need it later, too. The lower drawer was a mess of envelopes and paper, mostly overdue bills by the look of it. Dalton owed a lot of people money.

Joy was going through the filing cabinets. "These two are empty," she said, pointing to the ones on the right. "I guess Dalton wanted to look busier than he really was. This one has case files, but who knows if what we're looking for is here? Especially since we don't even know what it is."

"Is there a file for Hooke?" I asked. It was the only thing I could think of. It could certainly fit the requirement of being concealed in a drawer. And it would make sense the dead guy was here looking for it.

"Hard to say," replied Joy. "There doesn't seem to be any system here. I don't see a folder that says 'Hooke', but it could be filed under 'M' for 'Murder', 'S' for 'Smut', or 'D' for 'Dead body in the waiting room, and why the heck are we still here?'"

I leaned back in the chair and swiveled gently left and right some more to try to focus myself. She was right. We had no idea what we were looking for or what we were doing. This was the one idea I had, and it was a dead end. Literally.

Joy cocked her head sideways. "You're pale. We should probably get you some fresh air." I raised my hand and watched it tremble, and realized I must look as bad as I suddenly felt. Apparently, trembling was what my body did when it was stressed. We went out quietly, me leaning on Joy for balance, leaving everything the way we had found it except for the rye in my bag and the diary under my arm. Joy set the latch on the outer door before pulling it closed behind us. The elevator was back on the first floor, the old man asleep in his chair, so we took the stairs and left without waking him.

Chapter Five

Joy decided we both needed another drink to settle our nerves. She drove us back to Jack's bar, anxiously watching every speed limit, stop sign, and red light. The last thing we needed was some overzealous cop asking us where we were going and where we were coming from. Joy found a parking spot close by the bar. We stepped into the darkness inside and immediately the smells of old beer and other people's cigarettes hit my mouth and nose. Bile welled up in me and I could feel my stomach's contents floundering like a small boat in rough seas. "I need to go outside right now," I told Joy. "I feel nauseated."

Joy followed me outside where a few breaths of fresher air steadied me. "Let's walk for a bit," I said. We headed east with no particular destination in mind.

As we waited to cross at the next corner, I took Joy by the elbow. "Thanks. These last couple of days have been a lot more excitement than I'm used to."

"Hey, no problem, kiddo!" she told me cheerily. I didn't know if she was handling this better than me or just hid it better. And I put aside "kiddo" for later; at most she was a couple of years older than me.

"That was all a bit of a shock," I said. "I didn't think we would be the first there, but I thought we'd at least have the place to ourselves."

Joy didn't laugh. Maybe it wasn't as funny as I thought. "How you figure that scene?" she asked.

She probably didn't know it, but getting me to focus on rational hows and whys was the best thing for me. "We know a few things. One, the dead guy wasn't in the office for long before he was killed."

"Where do you get that?"

"Because he hadn't searched the office. The desk diary would have been the first thing he'd have taken. Two, it looks like what killed him was a blow to the back of the head. No wounds on the front. Plus, there was no sign of a fight, so it happened suddenly. So… possibilities. One, the guy goes up intending to ambush Dalton, but when he arrives Dalton is already there and gets the jump on him from behind. Which must mean Dalton knew him and expected trouble."

"I don't believe Dalton would kill a guy just like that!" said Joy, throwing her hands up.

"Not on purpose, perhaps, but maybe he hit him harder than he intended. Or the guy came through the door holding a gun."

"And then helpfully turned around so Dalton could hit him on the back of the head? What else you got?" she asked.

"Scenario two: maybe somebody else is already there when our dead man arrives, staking out Dalton's office in case he shows up. He hears the other guy coming, hides behind the door, and jumps him. Except it isn't Dalton, he realizes the guy is dead, and he leaves right away, making sure to leave no sign he was there and locking the door behind him."

"I like that better. The dead man could even just be a customer who showed up at the wrong time."

"That would be unfortunate," I said. "Or three, he was a potential customer who came in looking for Dalton, tripped on the rug, and bashed his head in on the coffee table." I took a beat. "And then locked the door behind himself before lying down and dying. No, I don't like it, either."

Joy stared at me for a couple of seconds, realized I was trying to make another joke, and gave a forced-sounding chuckle. "This is one hell of a puzzle," Joy said.

I tried to pretend I heard ladies curse like her all the time. I shook my head. "Not a puzzle. A mystery."

"There's a difference?"

"Sure. With a puzzle, you have everything you need; you just have to figure out how the pieces go together. With a mystery, there's facts you don't know and you can't solve it without them. I love puzzles. I hate mysteries. That's why I don't read Sherlock Holmes anymore."

Joy put a hand on my arm to stop me, and looked at me wide-eyed. "I love Sherlock! What's wrong with him?"

"The stories always cheat. The plot is always hiding some critical fact from the reader, something Holmes knows but you don't, and that's the key to the whole thing. Like an encyclopedic knowledge of the local railway timetable, or a type of mud only found in one place in north Essex. So you're trying to figure out a mystery while he's solving a puzzle and it's no wonder he gets there before you do. Sure, they're impressively constructed puzzles once you see all the pieces, but it just frustrates me. The reader never has a chance.

"If this were a Holmes story, the dead guy would have an imprint in his head that matches perfectly to the monkey-faced walking sticks carved only on a specific Pacific island, and the blow would have been struck where only a doctor would know it would cause rapid death. And Holmes would know both those things. And then in walks a neurologist lately returned from the South Seas."

"That's a lot of work to put into books you don't like," said Joy. I realized she was right, and filed her insight away for consideration later.

We'd arrived at a small park, just some open grass and a handful of small trees carved out of four empty lots in the middle of the block, two on the boulevard plus the two backing onto them from the next street north. In the center, benches were arranged in a hexagon around a modest river birch tree. Its distinctive, peeling bark made it one of the few trees I could identify without its leaves. Or with, for that matter. I was better at cars than trees. I asked Joy if she was okay if we sat for a while.

We lit cigarettes. I looked around to check we weren't being observed, and took a pull on Dalton's rye. I was embarrassed about drinking during the day, let alone in public, but I needed it. I offered it to Joy and she took just a sip. Suddenly, I found myself shivering. Joy put an arm around me and pulled me to her. My first reflex was to pull away - I've never taken easily to being touched - but after a moment, I forced myself to lean in and tried to relax into the hug.

I took a deep breath in and out to try to steady myself. "Thanks. You seem to be handling this a lot better than I am."

She shrugged and looked down at the grass. "Not my first dead body, I guess that's the difference."

Technically, it wasn't mine, either, but I knew what she meant. There was a chasm of difference between sitting at my father's hospital bedside while he quietly slipped away and stumbling over a violent, bloody death in the middle of somebody's office. "Oh. Wow." I said, wide-eyed and sitting up rigidly straight. "That's... is it something you want to talk about?"

She shrugged again. "There was an accident, a friend died, and I don't want to talk about it right now. I shouldn't have brought it up," she said abruptly.

I'm not adept at social cues as a general rule, but even to me it was obvious not to push on with the topic.

Joy exhaled hard and took another nip of rye. "Listen, we have to decide what to do about the dead guy," she said.

I tried to clear my thoughts. She was right, of course. "Here's what I see," I replied. "Sooner or later the police are going to find the body. If nothing else, it's going to smell bad soon. And when they do, they're going to talk to the elevator operator. And he's going to mention us, the woman and her girl cab driver. Which leads them right to you."

"Yeah, there's not a lot of girls still driving hacks these days," Joy replied anxiously.

"So maybe we should go to the police before they come to us?" I proposed.

"No!" snapped Joy harshly. "Sorry," she added quickly. "But no. I don't want any business with cops if we don't have to. We'd have to explain how we broke in and found the body, what we were doing there, the whole mess. And would you believe us? Because I don't think I would."

I couldn't disagree with her on that. "Then how about this way," I said. "We just wait it out. If they find us, our story is we went up there looking for Dalton, but the door was locked, and we left. That's all we know. I don't think they can tell I picked the lock, and there's no reason to doubt us."

"Yeah, that's better. And the elevator guy doesn't know how long we were up there, he was hard asleep when we came down."

I played it over in my head. "Good so far. Now they're going to want to know why we were there".

Joy looked bewildered. "Jesus and Mary, this is getting more tangled than a dimestore mystery magazine. Do you plan all your conversations ahead of time like this?"

"Actually, a lot of the time I do."

"And do they ever go the way you planned?"

"Almost never," I admitted. I'd have to add that to the pile of thoughts to pursue later. I returned to my narrative. "Anyway, I can tell them I was looking to hire Dalton and just happened to pick your cab. I was upset when we got there so you came in with me. I don't want to tell them why I needed a PI, and I didn't tell you, either."

She laughed. "Cabbies shouldn't have to give up their customers, anyway. Like priests and lawyers. Seriously, you wouldn't believe some of the stuff fares confess to us. And I just thought of one more thing. Maybe the guy from the elevator car saw who else went up. If he wasn't asleep again, that is."

"We should talk to him before the police do."

"Yeah. But listen, I can't run around like this all day, I have to work. There's probably a shift change for our elevator guy around seven or so tonight. How about I pick you up at the store before seven and we try to catch him on the way out?"

"Sorry, but there's something we have to do first. Do you know where Dalton lives? We need to check out his apartment. Things are going to move fast once the body is discovered, and we might not get another chance."

She gave me a look that might have been admiration. "Good thinking. I've been there plenty of times. We're going to need a key to get in - it's not the type of lock you pick with a couple of bobby pins - but I think I have an idea."

"I'm going to trust you." What did I have to lose?

"Are you still up for this? You looked terrible back there," Joy said, narrowing her eyes to peer more closely at me.

"Definitely. I'd much rather be doing something useful than sitting around the shop worrying and drinking. I am sorry about your shift, though."

She shrugged it off.

We walked back towards the bar in silence, both of us deep in thought, and picked up Joy's cab. I rode up front with her; sitting in the back had been making my nausea worse. On the way over, I briefly caught sight of a green Packard 200 with its unique grille and wondered if it was the same green Packard Joy had thought was tailing her, but it disappeared into traffic and I didn't see it again. I couldn't keep looking back without getting car sick, and after a few minutes, I gave up and put it down to coincidence.

It was a twenty minute ride to the apartment building Dalton lived in, an old but well kept-up redbrick building with stone accents which actually made architectural sense for once. Tall windows looked like they would let in a lot of light, and a lot of air, too, if opened. The neighborhood was also quieter than mine, and even had a few trees on the block. I was envious.

Joy easily found a parking spot nearby. A large but unpretentious door let on to a lobby, clean and well-lit, with a checkerboard tile floor and a large desk. Behind the desk was a set of cubby holes for mail, and an old, white man who hadn't shaved in a day or two, in his sixties, I guessed. Joy went over to talk to him while I stood back and waited.

"Hey Joe, I got a customer come to see Mr. Dalton. He said to wait upstairs for him, if that's okay?"

"That's fine, Miss D'Amico, here's his spare key," he replied in a hoarse baritone, a testament to a lifetime commitment to cheap whiskey and unfiltered cigarettes. He reached under his desk and came up with a large, warded key. Joy was right, it was definitely something I couldn't pick without much better tools. "Oh, and can you take his mail up? His box is getting full."

Joy took the stack of mail from him, letters of various sizes and a couple of magazines. There was no elevator, so we took the stairs to the fourth floor. We were both breathing heavily by the time we got there.

"Dammit," said Joy once we were out of sight of Joe. "I was kinda hoping..." but then she trailed off.

"Hoping for what?" I prodded.

"There's a trick for hiding something in plain sight. You put it in a package and mail it back to yourself, slowest way possible. Preferably from out of town if you can. When it arrives, you rewrap it and mail it again. As long as it's in the mail system, it's pretty much untouchable."

"Did you learn that from Dalton or from cheap detective novels?" I asked.

She laughed a little. "That's one of Dalton's, so I was hoping he might be doing that with whatever we're looking for. But nothing here could hold more than a couple of sheets of paper, and you already ruled that out."

She led the way to Dalton's apartment, unlocked it, and we stepped inside. We found ourselves in a decent sized room for a bachelor which seemed to serve as a combination sitting room and dining room. It was plainly and unfussily decorated, a single man's place. The room was neat; if anybody had searched it before us, they had put everything back afterwards. There were three doors from the room, two open. One led to a kitchenette, the one opposite it to a bedroom. The third, the closed door, had to be the bathroom. Against the far wall, underneath one of those tall, airy windows, stood a small, wooden table barely big enough for two to eat at, with two chairs pushed into it. It was clear apart from a single placemat. Joy left the mail on it.

Nearer to us were a red sofa and a large black armchair, arranged at right angles around the short and long sides of a low coffee table. In the angle between the sofa and chair was a side table with a chess game in progress on top. I looked closer: no, not a game; a puzzle. I resisted the urge to solve it and tried to focus on the job in hand. Together we looked at the papers spread out on the table, but they were disappointing. It was quickly clear they were something to do with a case in progress, a divorce. Hardly motive for kidnapping a detective.

There was a bookcase against the wall where we had come in and I knelt down to see if anything jumped out as anomalous. I didn't expect an 1865 Vanity Fair, but I was hoping, just perhaps, for something incongruous squeezed between the novels. Meanwhile, Joy did a circuit of the room, peering behind the pictures hanging on the walls.

"What are you looking for?" I asked, perplexed.

"Either a wall safe or something taped to the back of a picture," answered Joy. "Cheap detective novels," she said before I could ask.

We both came up empty. Joy offered to take the bedroom next, which left me the kitchenette. It was barely big enough to cook in. Cheap wooden cupboards, a two burner stove, melamine countertops, and a half-size sink. It didn't take long to verify the cupboards on the wall didn't contain anything but plates and a couple of pots. The drawers were equally unhelpful. I checked the oven, too, just for completeness. I guessed the only thing ever prepared in that kitchen was coffee.

I was looking up and thinking that on top of the cupboards would be a good place to hide something out of sight but readily accessible for a man of Dalton's height, and trying to figure out how I could get up there, when I heard heavy footsteps in the living room. We really should have locked the door. I filed the thought away for next time. I quickly figured there was no point trying to hide; whoever it was could check every room in a matter of minutes.

I grabbed the initiative and stepped back into the living room. The man standing there was average height, maybe five eight. If I danced with him I wouldn't be able to wear heels. He wasn't about to ask. He was wearing a dark, double-breasted coat with a broad stripe that buttoned very high on the chest, a style that hadn't been fashionable for a long while now, along with a gabardine trench coat. His hair was very black, slicked back, perfectly groomed. His shirt was plain white, his tie solid black, and he was holding a gun on me. He didn't looked surprised to see me.

I had never had a gun pointed at me before, and it was surprisingly unsettling. I was more worried it might go off accidentally rather than him shooting me intentionally; that didn't seem like it would get him anything. I decided to throw him a curveball and see how he swung at it.

"Mr. Dalton?" I asked as politely as I could under the circumstances. The man shifted his weight from foot to foot and had to give it some thought. Uncharitably, I guessed giving things thought did not come naturally to him. Finally he made a choice.

"Yeah, that's me. What are you doing in my apartment?"

"Well, this is a fine way to greet a potential customer. I came here about a case I hoped you might take on, and your lobby man kindly said I could wait up here. I was in the kitchen looking to make a cup of coffee."

He chewed on that. "I guess that's okay. You alone?"

I was pretty sure he knew I wasn't, but he was still playing at being Dalton.

"No. A friend came here with me."

"Where's your friend? " he asked, glancing at the three doors and waving the gun around. "She hiding in the kitchen, too?"

I really wished he'd put the gun away. Or at least point it in one place. "She had to use the lavatory," I said. "She'll be right out." I couldn't think of a reason to admit she was searching Dalton's bedroom. He glanced over at the closed door.

"I need you to leave now. I'll send her down when she's done. Assuming her story matches yours, that is."

I didn't like that at all. I'd put Joy in a big jam. I didn't have a plan, but I tried to stall. "Please, I really need your help," I said in what was probably a hopelessly theatrical attempt at playing desperate.

He looked more than a little angry. He took two steps over to me and grabbed me firmly by the upper arm. I would have bruises the next day for sure, which was inconvenient because I had been planning to wear my short-sleeved dress. I struggled to break free from his grip as he steered me towards the door.

"I said to leave. Right now, lady," he said. There was no doubt now he was angry.

And then he screamed.

He went down on one knee. Standing behind him was Joy, something small and dark in her right hand. She slugged him with it just behind the ear and he crumpled to the floor, face down and out cold. His hair was mussed where she'd struck him, but he didn't seem to be bleeding. I looked at her wide-eyed. I had never seen such violence up close before. This really was turning into a day full of firsts.

With no little effort, Joy and I rolled him over and I checked his pockets. There was a wallet with a driver's license in it, but the name on it didn't mean anything to either of us. I put it back.

"He's right though. We need to leave right now," Joy said.

We did, pausing only for Joy to turn the lock on the door behind her. It would be an interesting problem for the unconscious man to solve when he woke up. I figured he could probably go down the fire escape. She stopped off in the lobby to return the key, telling Joe we had decided to see Dalton the next day at his office instead of waiting.

Once we were back in the cab and well away from the building, I turned to Joy. "I can't believe you slugged that guy in the head! What did you hit him with?"

She reached into her pocket and pulled out a blackjack.

"You sapped the guy?" I gasped.

"Sure," she shrugged. "And I hit him in the knee. That's going to be sore for days, but I needed to get him down low enough to hit him on the head."

"I'm not complaining about the result, but it was really shocking."

Joy just shrugged again. "He pointed a gun at you. And besides, he lied to you about being Dalton. That was rude."

"Why do you even have a blackjack? Is it legal?" I realized I was babbling.

"Sometimes men get handsy, they think their fare is buying them more than a ride. A sharp rap across the knuckles usually wises them up. Sometimes they need a bit more. And it's legal so long as I don't get caught with it."

"Do you still want to check in with the doorman tonight?" I asked, changing the subject without warning. "This has already been a heck of a day."

"For sure," she replied, "We can't wait. And before this is over, I'm going to teach you to say 'hell'. But right now I need to work my shift if I want to eat this week."

She dropped me at my shop with a promise to see me at seven.

CHAPTER SIX

The shop was mostly quiet again, and the residue of the day dragged like a dog that had to stop at every tree. By five, the afternoon rain had come and gone and dried up, and so had the customers. I kept the store open an extra hour anyway since I had nothing else to do. I read the diary for a while but nothing jumped out at me, and by six I was impatiently killing time, waiting for Joy to show up. I tried to read something by Jane Austen but soon realized I had read the same paragraph half a dozen times and still didn't know who had offended whom with their bad manners. Putting the book back on the shelf, I walked into my back office, and finding nothing there to distract me, I turned around and came back out again. Walking circles around the store, I rehearsed a little speech for our elevator man.

I was standing in the window watching the evening traffic when Joy finally pulled up outside fifteen minutes before seven. I came straight out. She waved off a middle-aged couple who thought they'd gotten lucky to find a rare cab on this stretch of the boulevard, and I slid into the front alongside her. Ten minutes later, we were parked in front of Dalton's anonymous office building again. Tense, neither of us had spoken on the way over and we remained silent as we waited. A few minutes crawled by before we saw an old black man with white hair and a stoop go up the front steps. He was wearing a worn, khaki-colored raincoat, frayed at the cuffs and the collar, and carrying a brown bag about the size of a couple of sandwiches as well as a flask I guessed contained a night's worth of coffee. I reflected that sitting alone in an office building all night was a tough way for an old man to make a living. A few more minutes passed before the old Mexican came out, swaddled in a faded gray wool coat.

As he passed the cab, I called out to him. "Excuse me, sir?"

He startled and clutched his own brown bag close to his chest, saw us in the car, and relaxed. His tips were in the bag, I guessed. He came close to the car. "I remember you two ladies. You came by this morning and I took you up to three. Didn't see you come down though, was resting my eyes for a couple of minutes." His voice was a rich baritone with the serious gruffness in it that only decades of cigarillos and tequila will earn you. Any Mexican accent he might once have had seemed long gone, but he still had the cadences. In another life, he should have been a radio announcer. I stepped out of the car, and Joy slid across the seat and joined me. I offered my hand.

"I'm Dot, this is Joy."

"Ángel," he returned.

"We, uh… listen, Ángel, we think the police might come by soon and we need a favor."

He stopped me. "Police already came by, about noon. A couple of detectives with hard heads and big guts. Interrupted my lunch, if you can believe it."

So much for my rehearsed speech. Now I was improvising. "What did you tell them? About us, I mean?" I asked anxiously.

"Lady, I didn't tell them nothing about nobody," he growled. "Maybe you don't know much about how the police treat Mexicans in this town, but I got no reason to help them," he said to my confused expression. "They weren't exactly respectful, either, but I stayed polite. You know why they were here? They didn't say nothing, just asked who came and went."

Joy and I exchanged glances, and she stepped in. "I heard from another driver there was a dead body found in Dalton's office." It wasn't a very plausible version of events in my mind, but Ángel was too shocked to care.

"Dios!" he exclaimed, and crossed himself.

"Not Dalton!" I quickly added.

"Mother of God, don't do that to an old man!" he replied. "You know, now I'm thinking I ain't seen Mr. Dalton all last week. I just guessed he was doing his coming and going at night. Is he alright?"

"That's why we came by in the first place," said Joy. "We're friends of his and we've been worried. Did you take anybody else up to the third floor lately? Anybody who stuck out?"

He paused to give it some thought. "There were two guys caught my eye, just yesterday. They both seemed pretty hinky, one right after the other, but I didn't think much about it at the time. Besides Mr. Dalton's office, there's an insurance man on three and a dentist, too, and others besides. Lots of visitors got reason to go up there."

That lined up with the state of the body we'd found.

"Do you remember what they looked like?" I asked.

"One was mostly ordinary looking, except he had very pale skin, even for an anglo, like he never went outside, and the whitest hair I ever saw on a young man." That was our dead guy, I thought. "The other came in a minute later, just after I brought the car back down to the lobby. He was big, even bigger than Mr. Dalton, but strong, not fat. It felt crowded with just the two of us in the elevator. Dark suit, tough looking, face like a boxer who stayed in the game too long. And a scar down the side of his face like somebody came for his eye with a blade and missed." He illustrated this by drawing his finger from the corner of his right eye down his cheek and past his mouth. "And believe me, this man looked like if you come for him, you better not miss. I saw him come down the stairs just a few minutes after. I didn't see the pale guy leave, but didn't think anything of it. I close my eyes a lot.

"Hey, maybe you ladies shouldn't stay too long," said Ángel suddenly. "The detectives said they'd be back to talk to Bernie, the night guy."

"Will he tell them anything?" I asked anxiously.

"Ma'am, black people in this town got no more reason to help the cops than Mexicans do."

Or taxi drivers, I thought, remembering Joy's reaction earlier. Was I the only person in the city who thought the police were the good guys?

Joy rummaged in her inside pocket and pulled out a dollar. She held it out to Ángel. "Hey, thanks for your help."

"That's kind, but you don't have to do that," said Ángel.

"Then call it a tip. For not taking us up to the third floor this morning." Joy smiled.

Ángel grinned, took the money, and added it to his bag. "Any time, ma'am. "

He left, and we got back in the cab. Joy looked at me. "A pale guy and a mean-looking, big guy. It sounds like our dead guy and his killer, but I don't know what we do with it."

"Another piece of the puzzle," I shrugged.

After the day we'd had, it didn't take any persuading for Joy to get me to agree to a drink before we went home. She returned the car to the garage and signed it in before we walked over to Jack's. Inside, there were just a handful of cabbies still drinking. I recognized a few faces; I still hadn't learned any names besides Madge, though.

We went over and said our hellos, but as soon as we had, Joy surprised me by leading me to a table of our own. "We might want to talk business," she offered by way of an explanation.

We sat down, clinked our glasses, and lit our cigarettes, her usual Lucky Strikes and my Kools. A haze of smoke settled over the table.

"Hell of a day, huh?" said Joy.

"Heck of a day," I replied. "Let's take inventory. I flicked through the diary, but at first glance it doesn't tell us much. I need to think about it more."

"What are you looking for?"

"Patterns. And more importantly, changes in patterns. Like, was there somebody who Dalton was meeting with or a place he was regularly going, but it suddenly stopped? Or diary entries that don't have much detail, like he didn't want to put it in writing."

"Okay, something else," said Joy. "I'm gonna say for sure we're being tailed. I'm not imagining the green Packard, I saw it again when I was working today, and it matched me turn for turn for five blocks. And I think the guy I sapped was the driver. "

"We also know there's at least two people looking for whatever we're looking for," I replied. "And one of them is dangerously violent. It's a fair guess the green Packard is working for one or the other of them. Otherwise, we have three rivals in this snipe hunt, and that's too much coincidence for my taste."

"What about the guy at Dalton's apartment? Do you think he followed us there?"

I had to think for a moment and play out a couple of versions of events in my head. I took a couple of sips of rye to see if it would help. "I'm having a hard time coming up with something that makes sense. It sounds unlikely he would be there at the same time as us if he didn't follow us, or maybe he was staking out the place and saw us go in and then he went up. I guess he couldn't get in without a key, at least not without attracting a lot of attention. But either way, why interrupt us if he could let us do the searching for him? The smart move for him would have been to wait for us to leave with anything we found and hold us up for it the first chance he got."

"What if he just isn't very smart?" riposted Joy. "Most people don't think things through the way you do."

I chewed it over a little. "Fair enough. My first impression was he certainly wasn't the smartest cookie. So what's your version?"

"Suppose he's waiting at the apartment in case Dalton shows, watches us go inside, then comes close enough to peer through the door. He sees me get the key, and when we go upstairs, he panics. He hasn't thought about how much easier it would be to shake us down on our way out, so he gives us a couple of minutes' head start and follows us up."

"Good so far. But he tried to throw me out and keep you there," I pointed out.

"Yeah, but remember in my story, he doesn't really have a plan. Unlike you, he's making it up as he goes along. So maybe he thinks, trying to keep a gun on both of us could get complicated, and he only needs one of us to find the thing for him while he watches. And if he really bought that you mistook him for Dalton, he thinks you're not going to call the cops, at least not right away, so he lets you go. But he has to do something about me because I'll know he isn't Dalton."

"Still okay, I suppose. It wasn't smart of him to try to split us up, but we already agreed he's no Einstein. It's just really hard for me to think illogically. So what then?"

"Then he plans to put the gun on me and make me search the place for him. These guys still think we know what we're looking for and where it could be." She paused for a long draw of beer. "That could've gotten nasty if he thought I was holding out on him."

"Either way, he underestimated you. Badly."

"Yeah," said Joy, grinning. "I get that a lot." She took our glasses and stepped over to the bar for refills.

She had just set our drinks in front of us when I noticed one of the drivers get up from the table and head towards us. He was a little above average height, slim, and simply but neatly dressed, his shirt buttoned all the way to the collar. He had a wide-open face, blue eyes, and blond hair; modestly handsome in a Midwestern way - or at least how I always imagined Midwesterners. My experience outside Los Angeles was extremely limited, so I relied on Hollywood to know what the rest of the country was like and how its peoples looked. His hair was cropped as though he was recently out of the army, or perhaps he just liked to keep it short. He looked like he was in his late twenties, which could be misleading if he had seen combat. Some young men had seen things that had aged them quickly, and they rarely wanted to talk about them.

He came over and stood next to our table, nervously shifting his weight from side to side. "Uh, hi," he said.

"Dot, this is Mikey," said Joy. "He wanted to ask you a question. And I have to go fix my make-up." She got up from the table and headed towards the ladies' room.

I watched her disappear out of sight and realized Mikey was still standing, silent and nervous, waiting for me to speak next. "Sure, Mikey," I said. "What can I help you with?" I tried hard not to sound like the professional version of myself, but it was always difficult with strangers.

"Uh, well, I was wondering…" he paused and charged ahead. "I was wondering if you would go out with me one evening. You know, like a date?"

My whole body lurched like I'd missed the last step coming downstairs. "Like a date, or actually a date?" my inner pedant demanded out loud, buying me time. This was unfamiliar territory for me and I was afraid I was doing it very wrong, but I needed both clarity and a moment.

"Uh, definitely a date."

"That would be really nice," I said before I could give myself a reason not to. Just for once in my life, I thought, I'm not going to overthink this. "Is right now too soon?" I suspected it was unconventional, but I didn't want a chance to back out.

"Right now would be great," he said, his words tumbling out one on top of another like a clown car when the doors open.

"Good. Do you have a car?"

"Is it okay if I pick you up in a cab? I don't have a car of my own."

"That would be perfect. Joy has taught me to love riding in cabs. But you have to let me sit in the front seat."

He grinned happily. "I'll bring it around the front. Take your time finishing your drink."

We stared at each other for a few moments, both apparently unsure if there was anything else to say, before he turned and walked quickly back to join the other drivers. He mumbled a few words to them too soft for me to hear, and headed for the door. I shuffled my chair around so I couldn't see their table, and they couldn't see my face, which I suspected was rapidly reddening. Joy chose this moment to return, making me suspect she had been watching.

"Everything okay?" she asked, smirking.

"Mikey and I are going on a date," I said. "But I think you already knew that."

"Yeah, kinda. Right now?"

"Right now, before I get cold feet."

"Good. He asked me if it would be okay to ask you. I told him you'd love it. I think you two will get along."

"I do love it. Honestly, I have not been on a proper date since college, and I'm not sure those even counted."

"What was wrong with the college dates?" Joy asked.

"I went to a women-only college," I said. "And the local men's colleges had dances on Fridays and Saturdays. There were lots more men than women, so you'd have to be pretty hopeless not to get asked. Mind you, none of the men were what you would call great catches. I didn't care, though. I just loved dancing. And once I got a reputation for being pretty good at it, I could pick and choose my dance partners."

I picked up my rye, hesitated, put it down again, and looked her in the eye. "Look, are you really okay with this?" I asked anxiously. "You weren't hoping he'd ask you out, were you?" I could inject anxiety into almost any situation.

"Nah. Two things you should know about me. One, if I want a date with somebody, I don't wait for them to ask. I'll let them know straight up. And two, I would never date another driver. It would get so awkward afterwards."

"In any case, I bet you get asked out plenty. You're pretty, outgoing, independent. Am I right?"

"Oh sure, I get dates," said Joy, but she didn't seem too happy about it. "It's keeping a boyfriend that's hard."

"But why?"

She looked at me for a few long seconds. "Long story for another time. Sorry. You have a date to go on." I felt like Joy had a lot of stories that wouldn't come out until we knew each other better.

We lit fresh cigarettes and sipped our drinks in a silence that, for once, was awkward. Thankfully, Mikey soon pulled up in front and honked his horn, rescuing us.

I climbed in up front and Mikey drove us around for a while, going nowhere in particular and neither of us saying much beyond small talk, just both of us trying to unstiffen our shoulders and feel our way. We cruised over to Hollywood to see what new movies were on the theater marquees, but it seemed like a pretty rotten bunch of second-rate cowboy movies and murder mysteries.

Mikey shared a theory that all the top stars had been tied up for the past year making war movies, and now the war was over, nobody wanted to see those. So the studios had dumped a bunch of B pictures into theaters while they retooled for peacetime. We kicked it around for a while, making up titles for a really bad cowboy-murder-mystery movie, and I was delighted to discover we shared a sense of humor. It seemed like a good moment to breech a question I'd been burning to ask.

"Why do they call you Mikey? Why not just Mike? Childhood nickname?"

"Oh, it's nothing special. When I started, there was already a driver called Mike. So Madge called me 'Mike E.' when she did roll call - my last name is 'Eastman'. And pretty soon 'Mike E.' became 'Mikey'. I don't mind it."

I didn't mind it, either. "How long have you been driving?"

"Not long," he said. "I was driving for a few months before the war, but right after Pearl Harbor, I signed up for the army. I didn't want to wait to be drafted. I came home in '44 and pretty much right away went to get trained as a car mechanic on the GI Bill. Then I started at Red Star, driving and making some extra scratch as a mechanic on the side. To be honest, I like the fixing better than the driving." He hadn't said anything about what he'd done in the war, nor why he'd come home, and I'd learned that when a man does that, you let it lie. The reasons were never good.

"What about you?" he asked. "How did you come to be running a bookstore so young?"

I turned sideways in my seat so we could talk more easily. "Short version, I inherited it from my father. You want the long version?"

"Sure," he replied. "Give me the whole life story."

"Okay. I was born here in LA. My mother died when I was eight so I lived alone with my father. No brothers or sisters. I did well in high school, and my father figured out a way to afford college for me. I went to a small women's school on the south side of the city for two years until the war started. Then the Army started coming around looking to recruit girls who could do administrative work - real work, not just typing and filing - to free up men to go overseas, and I signed up." This last part wasn't exactly a lie, but it wasn't the whole truth, either. It would do for now. "It was fun and it helped the war effort. Anyway, it all came to an end when my father died."

"I'm sorry," interjected Mikey, and I felt like it was more than just a reflex.

"Thanks, but I have to say, we weren't exactly close. He'd wanted a son, and both my mother and I had disappointed him in that respect. But in fairness, he did the best he could to raise a girl while running the store. And he tried to get me an education. Anyway, when he died he left the bookstore to me with a request I keep it going. And two years later, here I am, barely making ends meet and wondering how much longer I can keep it up."

That was a lot more confessional than I had planned. And a lot more downbeat. There was something genuine about Mikey that made me want to open up to him. And made me hope he'd do the same in return. By now, we'd circled back around to downtown.

Mikey looked at me. "Do you like to dance?"

I looked down at my clothes and realized purely by chance I was wearing the perfect skirt for dancing: swishy, easy to move in, and not likely to embarrass me if I got too energetic. I think I must have smiled broadly because he did the same.

"I know a place, it's a bit small but it's pretty cool."

"Don't call it 'small'," I said. "Call it 'exclusive'."

He liked that.

We turned off the boulevard, down a couple of side streets, and he parked up. The street looked like brick warehouses for the most part, except for one door about fifty feet up the street with a brightly-lit marquee and a neon sign above. As we got close, I saw the sign simply said "Swing!" in green and purple letters.

Just inside the door, a small room did double duty as ticket booth and coat check. Mikey paid for us both and led the way down a narrow corridor which opened onto a room bigger than I was expecting from his description. In the center was a parquet dance floor, well used, judging by the shoe marks on it. Off to the left and right were scatterings of round tables, eight or ten on each side. Most of the tables looked occupied; if we wanted to sit, we'd probably be sharing a table with another couple. Joining the two sides were a bar at one end and a small bandstand at the other. It was a dance hall distilled to its bare minimum, and I loved it.

On the bandstand was a jazz five piece: saxophone, clarinet, trumpet, double bass, piano, all fronted by a torch singer in a low-cut scarlet dress looking like she'd been sewn in and would have to be cut out at the end of the night. How she could breathe, let alone sing, was a mystery to me.

Judging by the ripples of applause, she had just finished a number. She announced that she was taking "a short break" but the band would continue without her. As she disappeared into the back, the band launched into a cleverly minimal arrangement of Miller's Moonlight Serenade: big band music for small bands, I supposed. Mikey offered me his hand and led me out onto the floor. It was a good song to feel each other out to, slow and steady with a few flourishes, a chance to get to know each other's style.

Mikey started us out with an easy foxtrot step, and it was immediately obvious that he was going to be a delightful dance partner. His lead was sure and firm and his hand in the small of my back readily let me know where he was going, yet left plenty of room for me to express myself. We quickly relaxed into each other's movements. I double-stepped a tight turn under his arm, making my skirt swirl out, and moved in a bit closer. For a first dance, it was an unmitigated success.

The band segued directly into In the Mood and Mikey proved himself equally adept at up-tempo swing as he was at a slow foxtrot. That was followed by yet a third Miller song, the eminently danceable Tuxedo Junction. All three were songs I'd danced to frequently in college and felt thoroughly confident with; it couldn't have been better if the band had known I was coming. As they wrapped up and we applauded along with the other dancers, I realized we were both grinning. Nothing needed to be said.

The singer was coming back on stage now and Mikey suggested a drink. "The barman here mixes great cocktails," Mikey told me.

"I usually just drink straight rye," I replied.

"Can I get you to take a risk tonight?" he asked. I paused, decided to let go of my reliance on routine for one night, and nodded. He asked the barman for a Manhattan for me; for himself he ordered a Martini. We took our drinks to one of the tables off to the side and watched as other couples swayed their way around the room while the singer bled her heart out all over the floor to the tune of Cry Me a River.

I took a taste of my Manhattan and decided I had a new favorite drink; not that I expected Jack to know how to mix one, mind you. Mikey persuaded me to try a sip of his Martini and immediately I knew I would never be a gin drinker. Afterward, we sat quietly for a while. I liked the fact that Mikey didn't feel the need to fill every silence with chatter. To my surprise, I found myself hoping he'd take my hand. I thought about making the move myself, but decided that was more Joy's style. I didn't want to rush him.

After a couple of minutes he caught my eye. "Having fun?" he asked.

"More fun than any time since I left the army, I think," I replied happily. We took our time over our drinks and stepped out onto the floor again. Mikey showed off some fancy heel-and-toe footwork - he confessed to having taken tap classes as a child - and I gave him my best turns. We alternated drinks and dances, taking to the floor when it was more open and sitting out when it got crowded. Before I knew it, it was almost eleven, I was a confirmed Manhattan drinker, and Mikey was walking me back to the cab. We drove over to my apartment building, a feeling of contentment warming my stomach alongside my Manhattans.

I struggled to find the right words to express my happiness. What came out was good enough. "That was… really lovely. I don't ever say this, but you're very easy to be with."

"Thank you," he said. He might have been blushing ever so slightly; it was hard to tell in the darkness. "You, too."

I leaned in and kissed him on the cheek but decided that was wrong and, taking my courage in both hands, kissed him lightly on the lips instead. "Um, was that okay?" I asked as I pulled away.

"Very okay," he replied, definitely blushing now.

I leaned back in and kissed him again, just a touch more firmly this time. "Can we do this again sometime?" I asked.

"Sure," he said. "Is right now too soon?" It was a good line.

"Yes," I laughed. "But definitely next week."

"Okay," he replied. "And next time, let's get something to eat."

I realized we had completely forgotten to get dinner. I slid back across the seat, opened my door, and stepped out. He watched me all the way to the door. By the time I got up to my apartment and peeked out the window, he was gone.

It had been a very long time since I'd come home with my lipstick smeared. It felt good. I slept well.

CHAPTER SEVEN

Thursday morning arrived to wake me from the best sleep I'd had in a long time. I dressed in the same gray wool skirt and cardigan combo from earlier in the week but changed it up with a burgundy cravat. It wasn't my favorite color but it worked well with the gray. The skirt was long enough to hide a run behind the knee in today's nylons, which was something I hated having to think about.

I got to the bar before Joy, a few minutes before eight, and waited for her outside. I was raised to believe "on time" meant five minutes early, and like most of what I'd learned from my father, it was a hard habit to break. I was also excited about something I'd figured out and wanted to tell Joy as soon as I saw her.

A handful of minutes after eight, a cab pulled up across the street and Joy got out. It looked like she had been assigned another DeSoto today, but a different license plate from the one she'd had the day before. I hadn't thought about it before, but it made sense drivers didn't always get assigned the same car from day to day, just whatever was available when they checked in. She scuttled across the street between impatient commuters and joined me.

I pushed open the door and we stepped inside. We were immediately greeted with a round of shouts and waves from a group of drivers clustered around a table. I was surprised to see beers in front of them at this time of the morning. Joy explained it was the midnight drivers coming off shift. They lived upside down lives, she said, and always gathered for at least one quick beer before heading home to sleep through the day.

"If you think it's weird to pick up strangers in a car for a living, you ain't seen nothing in the daytime. Midnight shift is a special blend of crazy and dangerous. Once in a while I'd ride along with one of the boys just to see, but I'd never drive it alone. For sure, you get a lot of celebrities and they often tip well, 'specially if they want you to keep mum about where and when you picked them up. And if they don't tip, the gossip sheets sure will. And you get every kind of weirdo, sad-sack, loner, loser, and night owl in the small hours. Worst, though, is you also get a lot of drunks, and if you're not careful, a lot of cleanup at the end of the shift."

On cue, another driver came through the door behind us, tucked his hat under his arm, and zigzagged between tables, accompanied by a chorus of jeers and cheers, to join the group at the back. He pulled up a chair and squeezed himself in as a spare beer was pushed towards him. He took a long draw as if to wash away the taste and smell of whatever he had been cleaning.

As suddenly as yesterday, I was hit by a wave of nausea. I stepped back through the door into fresh air and sunlight, and Joy followed me, looking concerned.

"Sorry", I said, "I can't handle the bar this morning. Can we get coffee instead?"

Joy nodded, and I led the way to the next intersection and a block north to a place I frequented. As we walked, I wondered what I had even been thinking, agreeing to meet at a bar before breakfast. Was I really so eager to please? Or simply totally thrown off-kilter by the events of the week?

We took a table by the window, and I ordered black coffee and toast from a tired-looking waitress. Either she was just finishing up a shift or she had a long day ahead of her. Or maybe she remembered I was the weird woman who came in all the time but only ever ordered toast and coffee and tipped the bare, polite minimum. Fried eggs sounded good after a couple of days of too much rye, but I always tried to avoid food that could drip or spill. I didn't have enough good clothes to risk stains on any of them. I basically had three outfits that said 'professional bookseller' and I wore them pretty much in rotation. Joy ordered eggs over easy and the waitress poured coffee for her, too.

The coffee shop was small and basic, with seating for twenty people arranged in twos and fours around chipped and faded plastic tabletops, eight stools at the counter, and two more seats at a lone hightop. The chairs were just comfortable enough to tolerate for ten or fifteen minutes, either by design to keep customers from lingering or just because they were cheap. The dishware was mismatched melamine. The stuff was near-indestructible and seemingly everywhere since the war. The windows were dirty and I watched the outside world through a fog.

As soon as the waitress had poured our coffee and taken our order, Joy leaned into the table and looked intently at me. "Let's start with the really important stuff! How did it go with Mikey?"

"It was… delightful," I replied. "Is that the right word? He was just so easy to be with." I realized I was grinning again. "Thank you so much for setting us up."

Joy looked happy, too. "Yeah, I thought you two would make a good match. So dish the details!"

I shared everything, even confessing to the goodnight kiss. "I think we agreed to a second date," I concluded. "You're going to have to help me with the protocol."

The waitress picked that moment to return with our food.

"Right, let's talk business now," I said.

"Good! I think I know what we're looking for," Joy declared.

Apparently, my find would have to wait a few minutes more. "Okay, go."

"Dalton used to carry around a notebook about so big." She gestured, indicating something which would just about fit in a coat pocket. "Maybe half an inch thick. Black leather cover. Took it most places we went, pulled it out whenever we had down time, like a stakeout."

"So?" I asked. "He has a notebook. It doesn't sound unusual for a private eye."

"That's the odd thing. It struck me last night, he never wrote in it. He just read it, flicking between pages, and sometimes making a note in another book he carried, a smaller one."

"Then what's in it?"

"I don't know. He would never let me see a single page. He said it was too private. But I do know he came by it during the Hooke investigation. He said he'd slipped it into his pocket, thinking it might be important, and then hung on to it. Maybe it links everything that's going on to Hooke."

"Okay, sounds like something. I don't know what, though." I contemplated it quietly, trying to see where it fit. I thought I had only given it a few seconds, but it must have been much longer because I jumped when Joy spoke up.

"Hey, where'd you go, kiddo?" she asked.

"What do you mean?" I replied. I was still a little disoriented.

"You just went blank for a minute there, like you were staring at something on the horizon, and the horizon in here is a couple of miles past that brick wall."

"Oh, God, sorry. How long was I away?"

Joy gestured with her knife at the plate of half-eaten eggs in front of her. My coffee cup had been topped off, too.

"Sorry," I said again. "I can get like that when I'm thinking deeply about a puzzle. And sometimes I'll just sort of… wake up with the answer and not know how I got there."

"So it's a puzzle now?" asked Joy.

"Oh, it's still a mystery," I corrected myself. "But I think we're a couple of pieces closer to having a puzzle. A notebook that size vibes with the break-in. Small enough to hide in a secret compartment in the bottom of a drawer, too obvious to hide on a bookshelf. Of course, we still don't know why it's so important."

"No," agreed Joy. "But at least we know what it looks like."

I nodded. "I have something, too."

Joy added three spoons of sugar to her second cup of coffee and stirred. She ate the other half of her eggs while I talked.

"I went through the diary yesterday afternoon, and last night my brain came up with something while I slept." Joy looked at me like that was odd, but I let it pass. "Mostly it's scattered appointments with names and sometimes a note like 'divorce' or 'insurance fraud'. Nothing interesting. There were even a couple of appointments scheduled for this week and last, so if he disappeared of his own accord, he didn't bother to update his diary first. Nothing looked out of the ordinary, except for one thing: two or three nights every week for the past few months, it would say 'VT' and sometimes a location and nothing else. At first I couldn't figure it out, but then I realized it has to be the initials of the lady he's dating."

"Makes sense," said Joy between mouthfuls. I was terrified she might drip egg yolk on her shirt. "I never met her, never knew her name. Never even drove him to meet her. Classy society lady is all I knew. He kept work and personal business completely separate."

"I'm going to spend some time in the library and see if I can figure out who the mysterious VT was. Can we meet tonight at your bar? Say around six?" It sounded a lot more sensible to me than a breakfast meeting.

Joy agreed and took a last swallow of coffee before hustling out the door to her cab, leaving me to get the check. I guess I owed her. She picked up a fare almost immediately and was on her way.

I chewed my now-cold toast slowly and carefully, watching where all the crumbs fell. I paid the check, tipped as best I could from what little I was making, and walked the half-dozen blocks to the library. It was the best version of an LA morning: dry, slightly cool, with not even the slightest smell of rain in the air. A morning that made me briefly appreciate this crazy city.

The library was a two story Art Deco building covered in white stucco with arches over the windows and door purely for decoration, one of many built in the same style all across California during the Depression. Without the sign over the door, it could easily have been mistaken for one of the schools or post offices built around the same time, the government trying to create jobs and get people back to work. It looked big in comparison to the single story shopfronts making up the rest of the block, but as libraries go, it was quite modest. Nonetheless, it had the one thing I cared about: a newspaper archive.

I really didn't know what I was looking for beyond Joy's description of a "classy society lady", but the librarian at the reference desk was excited to help me after I told her I was a private detective researching a case, which was technically only a half-lie. I imagined the only people with less exciting lives than used booksellers were librarians. She led me down a corridor and through a reading room whose silence was punctuated by the sounds of hushed voices, stifled coughs, and echoing footsteps so unique to libraries, into a room mostly filled with bound volumes, the rest of the space taken up with a reading table.

She pointed me to the society gossip columns in a couple of the dailies and explained how they worked. She was about to give me a run-down on the recent gossip about her favorite Hollywood celebrities when another librarian demanded her attention, which was a lucky break for me. I started with yesterday's papers for no particular reason other than neatness and worked my way backwards. Each column was fairly short, a compilation of brief paragraphs for the most part, often little more than noting a certain society figure had been seen at a certain event wearing a certain designer's gown or, scandalously, the same gown she had previously worn to some other event. Apparently, this was interesting to many readers.

Others were written in a language I assumed would be familiar to regular readers, especially the pieces which were licentious or even borderline-libelous. I understood the purpose was to conceal, at least to the point of legal deniability, the target of the gossip. The librarian had explained to me about blind items, which sounded exactly like my type of puzzle. I quickly had my first hit:

A certain society heiress was seen on Saturday at Carlton's, but without the hunky beau who has been by her side her for the past few weeks. Is one romance over and a new one brewing for V.T.?

Not much help in identifying V.T. but it at least confirmed I was looking in the right place. I worked my way back two more weeks before I got another hit, this one a mention of V.T. with presumably the same "rugged but underdressed" escort hosting a group of friends for cocktails at the Marmont. The columnist seemed fascinated to know who he might be, as apparently he was not known in society circles. Another piece noted whenever they were seen together, she was the one picking up the check, and made some innuendo about the nature of their relationship whose meaning I could guess at. These columnists didn't seem to let anything go by without some sort of insinuation.

Finally, I found something useful. Miss Virginia Townsend had presented awards at a charity for former jockeys fallen on hard times, her first time undertaking the responsibility in place of her late father. The article mentioned she was a familiar sight mingling with the celebrities at the reopened Santa Anita, and noted she was being "supported" at this difficult time by an "attractive, unidentified man". They had to be talking about Dalton.

Surely, this was my "VT". From there, it was fairly routine to dig out the family history. Her grandfather had come west in the last century, struck oil, made his fortune, and built the family mansion in High Victorian style. Her father, the youngest of five children, had pursued a career in the cavalry before being forced into retirement with a bad heart. He had promptly married a much younger woman who died giving birth to Virginia, and then whiled away his remaining years pursuing a variety of hobbies and causes, none of them parenting, which was left to a parade of nannies, governesses, tutors, chaperones, and professional companions.

By the mere fact of outliving his siblings, according to the terms of their father's will, he came into sole possession of a decrepit mansion far too large for one man and his daughter. The mansion was now, in turn, the property of Miss Townsend. The gossip columnists speculated she had little interest in the place and would not stay there for long, and the speculation always mentioned some newly-arrived Hollywood star in search of an impressive residence who might buy it.

I put away the papers, gathered my belongings, and left. On my walk back to the shop, I formulated a plan to introduce myself to Miss Townsend. I very much doubted a direct approach based on having once briefly met Dalton would open doors. Instead, I decided to send her a note introducing myself as a bookshop proprietor and dealer in fine used books, which was partly true, offering my condolences for the loss of her father, and proposing to make an offer for her late father's library, should she be interested in selling. I would follow up with a phone call to make an appointment.

I assumed a large library of impressively-bound books would be a requirement of any Victorian mansion, and if the speculation was correct and she was planning to move, she might well be interested in getting rid of them. Once inside, I could gently broach the question of Dalton, and I spent the remainder of the walk rehearsing a speech which would open the topic, hopefully without immediately getting me thrown out.

When I reached the store, a man was waiting outside. He was as long and thin and brittle as a reed. He said good morning and tipped his hat, a light khaki-colored fedora with a dark green hatband, revealing fine, sandy hair which I expected would fall forward boyishly from time to time requiring him to sweep it back. He waited patiently while I unlocked the door. I stepped inside and he followed me in. I asked him to give me a moment to finish opening up. He nodded. I stepped into my office, closed the door behind me, and leaned against it while I summoned up my professional face and voice. I returned to the store. "How can I help you?"

"Miss Stone, I assume?" I nodded. I struggled to place his accent. I thought he might be trying for an English accent, but it sounded more like a bad impersonation of Cary Grant.

He handed me his card and I read it out loud. It said "Anthony Grayson," and underneath, "Entrepreneur".

"It's pronounced 'Antony'," he responded. "It's the British pronunciation," in answer to a question nobody was asking. I sized him up while I waited for him to make the next move. He wore a lightweight seersucker jacket but without the usual colored stripes; instead, it was a plain, off-white all over. It would have been ideal for a Los Angeles summer but seemed rather out of season in January. It was beautifully cut, though, fitting him in all the right places, and conservatively styled in defiance of this season's more exuberant trends in lapels.

His shirt was pale pink, lightweight cotton, the cuffs held in place by ostentatiously large gold cufflinks. He took off his hat and set it on top of a stack of coffee table books on the central table. I had to admire the way the jacket perfectly adjusted to his movements: I had seen army officers perform that same maneuver in their crudely-cut uniform jackets and winced as their sleeves ruched up at the elbow and bit them in the armpit. His tailor was clearly a genius and entirely wasted on men. His ankle boots were equally elegant, slim, light brown leather, highly polished, and I assumed hand-made. He looked like he could have strolled in from a safari, if safaris were air-conditioned.

"I believe you and I have an interest in common", he said, maintaining the faux-English accent. "A certain book."

"Vanity Fair, 1865?" I replied, just to see what reaction I might get.

He looked perplexed. "No," he answered archly. "I'm referring to something of greater significance, as I'm sure you know. Would you do me the courtesy of having dinner with me tonight so we can discuss it further?"

I was intrigued. I had no idea how Grayson fit into the evolving mystery, or even whether he was trustworthy. But maybe he could provide more puzzle pieces. I agreed. As to why he thought I knew anything, I had only guesses.

"Excellent!" he exclaimed. "I'll send a limo for you at six-thirty. Oh, and don't worry about dressing up, the restaurant is not overly formal." I wondered sourly what he imagined I owned that was more formal than my best working clothes.

"Anyway, I will leave you to your business for now," he said, gesturing theatrically at the otherwise-empty shop. He picked up his hat and left.

Outside, I watched him carefully seat his hat with both hands, turn sharply left, and disappear from my sight. I sat down behind my table and tried to fit Grayson's new information into the picture. It occurred to me Mr. Antony-like-the-British Grayson might be the one who had been having Joy tailed in the hope of being led to the notebook. Did it also mean he was holding Dalton? And was he responsible for the dead body in Dalton's office? Perhaps he'd also arranged the break-in at my store. My next reaction was maybe dinner wasn't such a clever idea, but I reasoned to myself if Grayson intended me harm, this was a very polite and elaborate way of going about it. And tonight might be a chance to elicit some answers.

Once my mind was settled, I called Madge and left a message canceling my meeting with Joy in the evening and asking her to meet me for breakfast again tomorrow instead.

I told the Madge where I was going, and asked her to tell Joy, too. It couldn't hurt to be careful. She said of course. With my backup plan in place, I started to feel the barest bit more comfortable.

I resolved to skip the note to Miss Townsend. Events were moving too fast, and I would just have to call her directly, despite my discomfort.

I spent the next hour working up to calling Virginia Townsend, finding small jobs to do around the shop, and serving a few costumers. The books on the display table were insufficiently squared off, and some ragged-spined paperbacks, too damaged to sell, had to be removed from the Romance section. Finally, I was ready. I asked the operator to connect me and waited, breathing slowly and deliberately to control my anxiety while the line rang. I counted six rings before a voice announced, "Townsend residence". It sounded like a genuine English accent; I assumed it was the butler.

I introduced myself as "Dorothy Stone", believing it sounded better for the role I was attempting than "Dot", and explained I was a book dealer, I had heard Miss Townsend planned to sell the house, and would like to arrange a meeting with Miss Townsend to discuss acquiring her father's library. The butler asked me to wait for a moment. I heard receding footsteps followed by silence; presumably he had gone to ask for instructions. I doodled aimlessly on my notepad while I waited.

After a couple of minutes of silence, other than the sound of my own heart pounding in my ears, I heard the receiver being picked up and the English voice asked me if I might be available at nine o'clock the next morning. I immediately agreed. I hung up and exhaled. I was stunned I was getting a meeting so soon and so easily, but I wasn't about to complain.

Chapter Eight

The so-called limo wound its way east, up one of the canyon roads north of Route 66. The car was disappointing to say the least. When Grayson had promised a limo, I was expecting something like a Packard or a Cadillac, but instead, it was just a stretched DeSoto; it might even have been a repainted former taxicab, judging by the sagging of the back seats. The driver was equally disappointing. He was a ferret-faced, jittery man in a cheap black suit, shiny at the elbows and knees, and no hat. The suit coat fitted him so poorly I wondered if it were borrowed. It all seemed incongruously at odds with the impeccably put-together image Grayson himself projected.

My driver's handling on the switchback road did not fill me with the confidence one normally gets from professionals, alternating between scarily fast on the straightaways and maddeningly slow on the curves, punctuated by surging and braking. The view down into the canyon would have been spectacular in the hands of a more competent chauffeur; with him, it was not a direction I wanted to look. I was starting to feel carsick and tried to focus as far ahead as the winding road allowed. The driver didn't speak, which left me plenty of time to worry about how I was going to handle the meeting. Grayson obviously thought I knew more about Dalton's notebook than I really did, so I would have to be careful.

I didn't know the area at all but guessed we'd crossed over into San Bernardino county a while back. The sun was setting behind us, and every time we came out of the shade of a bluff, it threw an enormously elongated shadow of the car ahead. Behind, the landscape was lit in red turning to black. Eventually, we turned into a driveway and pulled up in front of a valet station, behind which stood a large, white-stuccoed ranch style building with a terracotta tiled roof. I waited a few moments for the driver to come around and open my door, but realized he wasn't going to and let myself out.

As soon as I had closed the door behind myself, he pulled away around the side of the building to a gravel-covered area where two dozen or more other cars were already parked. I walked up the steps to a pair of large mahogany doors detailed with brass fittings where a distinguished-looking doorman in a long, gold-braided coat and matching hat waited to open one of them for me, touching his fingers to his cap as I passed through.

Inside, the large semicircular foyer was spectacular, if one wanted to be kind about it. The lower half of the walls was white paneling, the upper half crimson and gold wallpaper all the way up to the twelve foot high ceilings. There were gold flourishes on the rosettes where the panels met, and more gold on the corbels at the joins of the cornices. The pictures on the walls, clumsy landscapes coarsely imitating the Hudson River school, were also heavily framed in gold. An outsized gold and crystal chandelier hung above the center of the room. Whoever had decorated the area certainly had a theme in mind, and it wasn't 'elegant restraint'.

Five doorways let off the foyer, the two to the left with brass plaques indicating lavatories; the two to the right were unlabeled, and I assumed were private offices. Either that or janitorial closets. In the center, a pair of double doors was open to the dining room from which emanated a low murmur of conversation and the staccato tinkles of formal dinner service. To their left stood an elaborate, wooden lectern, and behind a hostess of striking elegance.

She was everything the room was not, wearing a simple and probably wildly expensive black silk dress that fitted everywhere it should and moved whenever she did, complemented by a modest pearl choker and matching pearl earrings, her raven-black hair up in an elaborate arrangement which almost certainly required help. She wore just enough makeup to emphasize her large, hazel eyes, prominent cheekbones, and Cupid's bow lips, the type of natural beauty that takes thirty minutes to apply.

As I walked over to her, she smiled welcomingly, exposing perfect teeth. Her face almost, but not quite entirely, hid her opinion of my outfit. I told her Mr. Grayson was expecting me.

"Of course, Miss Stone," she said, and conducted me to a booth with a good view of the rest of the room. She told me Mr. Grayson was just taking care of some business and would be along shortly. She beckoned over a waiter in a white dinner jacket and whispered to him just loud enough for me to overhear, "Mr. Grayson's table". He nodded, and she walked away.

He promptly brought me a glass of water, took my order for a Manhattan, and left two menus on the table. The menu in front of me had no prices on it, so I picked up the other one. At a glance, I figured a decent meal would cost about as much as my store took in a week. I put it back on his side of the table.

Grayson had still not arrived, so I took the opportunity to check out the room. The decor continued the lobby's theme of "too much gold" up its walls, onto the ceiling, and around the chandeliers. There were no more than twenty widely-spaced tables and booths, about half of them occupied by couples and foursomes. You could certainly have a conversation here without fear of being overhead. The men, all of them late middle-aged or worse, wore dark suits and plain ties, apart from a handful who had opted for black tie. The women wore a variety of gowns, laden with bows, ruffles, frills, flounces, gathered skirts and ruched bodices, in a range of colors and patterns, most of which I considered would have looked better on drapes than dresses. By comparison, I was distinctly underdressed.

The women divided fairly obviously by age into First Wives and Second Wives; the two couples at the table nearest me included one of each, with the First Wife bearing a constant scowl at the fluttering over-attentiveness of the Second Wife to her recently-acquired husband. When the Second Wife reached over to taste something off of her husband's plate, I was fearful for one moment the First Wife was going to pin her hand to the table with a dessert fork and explain the niceties of formal restaurant etiquette to her, but fortunately, the moment passed without incident.

Grayson chose that moment to slide into his seat opposite me. He had changed into a linen suit a few shades darker than the seersucker he had been wearing earlier. His face obviously registered that I had not bothered to change, but he offered no comment.

"Good evening, Mr. Grayson," I said. "This is a lovely restaurant." My heart was thumping like the hooves of a thoroughbred rounding the last bend at Santa Anita at the prospect of carrying off the risky conversation, and I was doing my best to appear calmer than I felt.

"Thank you," he said with his faux Cary Grant affectation. "Didn't I mention? I own it," he explained, noticing my confusion. "It's one of my favorites among my business ventures."

"I'm sure we'll get excellent service then, Mr. Grayson," I said awkwardly. I immediately wished I'd said something smarter. Or just smiled and said nothing at all.

"Always," he replied. "And please, call me 'Antony'. That's the Brit--"

"I know," I interrupted. I thought for a flash he looked angry, but it passed so quickly, I wasn't sure.

His face resumed its equanimity. "Shall we order?" he asked. "I hope you've had a chance to look over the menu. I'm quite familiar with it, of course. And I hope you don't mind if we have my usual wine?"

I didn't care what wine he ordered, I was planning to stick to what I knew I liked. The waiter appeared, although I hadn't seen Grayson give any signal more obvious than a raise of the eyebrows. I guessed they were pretty well trained. He took our orders and vanished as smoothly as he had arrived.

As usual, I had picked out items I hoped offered the least risk of splashing anything on my outfit, which I would need to wear again on Monday. With all the time I'd left the shop closed during the week, I definitely could not afford to have it cleaned. We made small talk over salads, or rather he did. I listened patiently and nodded appropriately and murmured approval from time to time as he talked about some of his other businesses: a jazz club, a wine bar, a smaller and less formal restaurant in Beverly Hills, what he referred to collectively as 'hospitality'.

Once the salad plates had been cleared, he broached the real purpose of our meeting. "Let's talk about the notebook," he said. "I need to recover it."

"Why?" I asked, more in hope than expectation. I thought it was surely going to be difficult extracting information from him without letting on how little I knew.

"Because my name is in there, and if it fell into the wrong hands it would be very damaging for me, both personally and for my businesses," he confessed.

What did he mean? Was it a ledger of his businesses revealing fraud? Something personal, perhaps exposing embarrassing peccadilloes? I filed the thought away for future examination. I took a risk and hung out some bait. "And you're willing to pay for it, I take it."

"Would five hundred dollars be appropriate? Plus any expenses you incur, of course."

Five hundred would solve my financial problems for at least a couple of months.

"If I told you I don't know where it is, what would you say?"

"I'd say you and your taxi driver friend were holding out on me for more money, or because you want to run the business yourselves. The latter would be a big mistake, I assure you."

"Why?" I asked. This was not going well.

"An operation like that needs protection, especially given some of the people involved. You'll make some powerful enemies. Look what happened to Hooke. And who knows what has happened to Dalton? Some very nasty people will try to take the book off of you."

Was Grayson implying that Dalton had been kidnapped, like Joy imagined? If so, would delivering the book to Grayson leave Dalton dangling in the wind? What if he'd been kidnapped by somebody other than Grayson? And that was assuming I could even find the book. Too many what-ifs. I hated mysteries.

"If I can get you the book, what will happen to Dalton?"

"Presumably once the book is located, nobody has any reason to continue holding him. Assuming that's what has happened to him, of course. There's always the possibility he's just lying low, hoping this will all blow over, leaving him in possession of the book."

I tried to persuade myself that no longer holding Dalton could only mean releasing him, not disposing of him. I was not very convincing. "Alright. If I can find the book, I will deliver it. For five hundred dollars and the safe return of Dalton. But I promise you, I really don't have it right now." I didn't know whether or not he believed me. I was beginning to suspect I had created a horrible mess for myself.

"And I promise you, I don't have Dalton," he replied.

I had no reason to doubt him, other than the fact that I didn't believe a single word he had told me.

"He's an odd bird, by the way," he continued. "Nobody seems to know anything about him. Do you trust him?"

"I don't think I need to," I replied.

Conversation paused for a moment as our entrees were served. I was convinced now that Grayson had some means of signaling our waiter, and had held him off until the discussion was concluded. A lot of people are careless about talking in front of hired help, but Grayson was apparently more cautious. It was time to dive into some other difficult topics.

"By the way, do you have a car following Joy?" I asked. "A green Packard?".

He had the grace to blush ever so slightly. "The girl cab driver? I confess, those are my people. I was hoping to talk to her about the notebook, but honestly I have found you a lot easier to deal with."

"And do you have a big guy working for you, with a face that looks like he went a few too many rounds in the ring?" I repeated Angél's gesture. "Scar from here to here?"

This time, he looked visibly concerned. "That would be Sal Moretti. He works for a man named Accardo. Have you run into him?"

I ignored his question, feeling as though for once I had the initiative. Another piece had clicked in to place: it seemed Grayson and Accardo, whoever he might be, were the two parties after the book. I wondered what else was in it. "What about an average-sized guy, white hair, complexion like he doesn't get outside a lot?"

"Whitey Boyle. Yeah, he's mine. What about him?"

"You know he's dead, right?" I asked conversationally, as one does between dinner companions. I watched closely for a reaction.

I got less than I hoped for, just a small surprise, not major shock. "How do you know that? The police have kept it out of the papers so far, at my request."

"I have my own sources," I lied. "What if I told you Moretti killed him?"

This time, he did look shocked. "The police didn't tell me that," he said; I thought he sounded shaky now.

"The police don't know yet," I replied. "But I thought you should. A professional courtesy, if we're going to do business together."

He looked deep in thought. "Okay, this could be a problem."

"Why?" I prompted him again.

"You don't know who Accardo and Moretti are, do you? They were sent out here by the Chicago Outfit to clean up the mess in Hollywood. Brains and muscle. I do some business with them, not all of it by choice."

It didn't mean much to me; I guessed Grayson was once again assuming I knew more than I did, but my gambit of offering up Moretti as Boyle's killer did seem to be paying dividends. Maybe Joy could translate it for me later.

"What kind of business?" I pushed. I was fascinated to see how much he was willing to tell me in exchange for my one morsel. Or perhaps he thought I would be impressed by his underworld connections.

"For one thing, they run all the laundry for the hospitality businesses. They're ridiculously expensive, but No is not an acceptable answer to their contract terms, if you understand me. On the plus side of the ledger, they provide me with contraband liquor for my restaurants and bars, which is a nice profit for me. I hope this incident isn't the beginning of something bigger that would interfere with our business relationship."

Somehow I wasn't surprised that he was more concerned about his business than the death of an employee. On the other hand, I was very surprised how readily he confessed to me about evading tax. His urge to brag, it seemed, overwhelmed whatever discretion he might have.

Our plates were cleared once again, and I declined dessert, accepted coffee. "I do have one more question for you," I said.

"Go ahead," he replied.

"Where's the casino?"

To my surprise, he only smiled; I was expecting him to be at least a bit more impressed. "Very clever. How did you figure it out?"

"Basically, the restaurant is too small, in both senses. There isn't enough revenue here…." I gestured at the room. "…to justify a business of this size, the decor, the high-end tableware, the staff. Not even at these prices. And second, this room is taking up only a fraction of the building. Even allowing for a kitchen, there's a lot of floor space unaccounted for. There's also too many cars parked outside for the number of people in here. Whatever else you're doing here isn't obvious, so probably illegal; but the customers have to plausibly look like they might be arriving for dinner. And it has to be profitable enough to carry all this cost. Therefore: casino."

"Let me show it to you," he said, rising from the table. I followed him back out to the lobby and to the nearer of the two unlabeled doors I'd noticed earlier. Opening it, we stepped into a wide corridor I judged ran the length of the restaurant, and at the other end a very large man with a white dinner jacket and a bad haircut waited to open another door for us. Inside was the casino; the space was at least as large as the restaurant. It wasn't Monte Carlo, but it was more than big enough to pay the bills.

"This used to be a speakeasy during Prohibition," explained Grayson. "Legitimate restaurant in the front; liquor and dancing in the back. After Repeal, it was just an unprofitable restaurant for a while, probably a front for money laundering. I acquired it a few years ago and installed the casino. It seemed like a natural fit."

At the tables, various games were being played or watched by small clusters of clients. The players were dressed more smartly than the diners, almost all of the men in black tie and the women in dresses I actually coveted. There was a hum of muttered and whispered noise, louder than the restaurant had been, overlaid with the rattle of roulette balls and the snap of cards being dealt, punctuated by the occasional cheer when, presumably, a particularly large or audacious bet paid off. There was a bar, too, and it was keeping busy. Legality aside, it was an impressive business operation, but my brain was nagging me that something else was still missing, and I hoped it would let me know soon what it was, because it felt like an itch in a place I couldn't scratch.

"Would you like to play?" asked Grayson. "House money, of course".

"Honestly, I don't see the point," I replied. "The only two games I understand are blackjack and roulette. Blackjack has a house edge of two per cent, and roulette more than five, even without rigging the games. I really don't see the fun in standing around all evening slowly losing money."

"To be frank, I agree with you," he replied. "That's why I'm running a casino, not playing in one."

"But why all the way up here in the hills?"

"Quite simply, the San Bernardino authorities are lot more understanding about this type of venture than the ones in LA. From time to time, the city gets a district attorney determined to make a name for himself by cleaning up corrupting influences, and it's very disruptive. San Bernardino has no such issues, provided the right people get paid and we look reasonably legit from the outside. Some pretty influential people like to play here too, which helps."

"I should be leaving," I told him suddenly. The constant hum of conversation, the staccato rattling of roulette balls, and the close-pressed crowds around the tables were registering in my brain as claustrophobia worse than a streetcar at rush hour. I felt as though I was being squeezed on all sides.

"Of course. I'll have my man drive you home. When can you get the notebook to me?"

"As I said, I don't have it. Give me a week to see what I can find." I had no idea whether it was realistic, but I had to make something up, and I had to get out of there before discomfort turned into full-blown panic. If I had nothing at the end of a week, at least I had time to come up with a stall.

I gave the ferret-faced driver an address a couple of blocks from my apartment; I really didn't want him or Grayson knowing where I lived. I spent most of the ride home picking the bones out of the conversation in my mind, still bemused at how the little information I had given Grayson had made him assume I knew much more, and consequently share so much in return. And worrying about how much trouble I had talked myself into.

The clock was ticking on locating the darn book.

Chapter Nine

Friday was a drab, gray morning, one that Los Angeles should be ashamed of compared to the rest of the week. I met Joy for breakfast at our coffee place again, and brought her up to date on Grayson while we ate. In return, Joy explained to me about the Chicago Outfit. She was as interested in real crime as fictional, it turned out, and apparently, there were magazines for it.

The Chicago boys were one of the most powerful organized crime gangs in the country, on par with the Five Families in New York, at least if you could believe the more sensationalist newspapers, she explained, and a few years ago, they had tried to move in on the Hollywood unions. It had not gone well. Several of them had landed in prison, including some top people, and now they were getting out and trying to restart the business.

My brain had also done some work for me overnight, and I had woken with a clearer idea of how the pieces might be starting to fit together.

"So what do you figure is in the book?" asked Joy, while chewing dangerously on her egg. I feared for her slacks.

"I'm pretty sure it's a collection of blackmail material, and when Dalton got hold of it, he decided to keep it to himself. Probably some of the names in there were Hooke's pornography customers, which is how he kept them quiet about the library. Maybe there are even some powerful people who helped to protect the business. Grayson claims he wants it because he's one of the blackmail victims, and I suspect Accardo wants to continue the business for himself. I assume Dalton was trying to keep it out of the wrong hands, if he's the good guy you say he is."

"Huh," said Joy. "Maybe Hooke wasn't killed over the pornography at all. Maybe one of the blackmail victims decided he didn't want to pay any more."

"Interesting angle," I replied. "And a bit worrying if they think we have the book now."

"So Moretti is the guy who killed Grayson's man?" asked Joy, returning to the topic at hand.

"We don't know for sure, but he fits the description, and Grayson didn't question it, so I guess Moretti has a history. The alternative is somebody else killed Boyle and Moretti just stumbled across the scene minutes later. That seems like far too much coincidence to me. But either way, he didn't hang around afterwards."

"But why kill him? Do you think maybe Boyle found the book and Moretti took it off of him?"

"I don't think that works. If Moretti had passed it on to Accardo, I'd think one of the first things he'd do is put the screws to Grayson, and then Grayson wouldn't be asking us to find it. So I don't think either of them has the book right now."

"Yeah, makes sense. Maybe Moretti just likes hitting people and he overdid it," said Joy. "I've told you before, not everybody makes smart decisions. But at least that's good news for Dalton."

"How so?" I asked. I hated how pretentious that sounded even before I finished saying it.

"Whoever gets the book, they don't need Dalton anymore. And I don't think they will just let Dalton go after kidnapping him. The only way Dalton gets out of this is if we get the book first and trade it for his release."

I let that marinate.

We finished our coffees and cigarettes, and Joy picked up the check this time. I couldn't recall whether that meant we were even or I owed her one. And then I thought, maybe not keeping accounts is a good working definition of a friendship.

We got in the cab, me sitting alongside her as usual. On the ride over to visit Miss Virginia Townsend, I kept an eye open for a green Packard. I didn't see it, but I did notice something else bothering me. I turned to Joy. "I think we have a tail, a new one. A black Nash 600. About half a block back, I've seen it make the last three turns the same as us."

"Half a block behind is the way Dalton taught me to do it. But that sounds like a pretty common car. Are you sure it's the same one each time?" Joy asked.

"Definitely," I responded. "This one has a crushed front fender on the passenger side. I noticed it on the last two right turns we made. That's going to be an expensive repair, by the way."

"What is it with you and cars anyway?"

"Ever since I was little, I've just had a thing about car models and years and details. My father used to go into dealerships and pretend to be a buyer just to get me a catalog. And, well, I have this trick memory that remembers pretty much everything. Can we lose them?"

"No problem," said Joy. "Here's a little routine Dalton taught me." She slowed her approach to the next light, letting it turn red as we got there. There was a car between us and the Nash, which Joy told me was supposed to make it harder to spot a tail. But right now it meant that they couldn't follow us as Joy made a right against the red light. She quickly made another right into a side street and pulled over.

"Quick, jump in the back," she told me. "Take off your cardigan and pin your hair up." As she talked, she reached under the passenger seat and pulled out a cheap-looking blonde wig and tucked her hair into it, tossing her cap on the seat.

"Okay, now we're a completely different cab," she smirked.

"But it's the same license plate," I objected.

"Kid, other people do not pay attention to details the way you do," replied Joy.

One of these days I would have to internalize that.

She pulled a quick K-turn and stopped the cab back at the intersection with the street we'd just turned off. We got there just in time to see the Nash sail past us, the driver and passenger looking urgently from side to side trying to find a cab with two dark-haired women sitting up front. I couldn't believe such a stupid gag had worked so well, but I didn't see the Nash again the rest of the way to the Townsend mansion.

It took us another fifteen minutes to reach the estate, just outside the city limits. Large, black-painted wrought iron gates in High Victorian style were set into a brick wall that sagged and crumbled in places. The gates stood open. The way the gateposts leaned, I wasn't sure they could be closed, even if somebody wanted to. Possibly original to the house, I thought.

We turned in to the moneyed sound of gravel crackling under our tires. The driveway took a long curve, lined by plane trees, so the house itself didn't come into view until we were fifty feet inside the gate. It was a Victorian pile in red brick with sandstone around the windows and, like the wall, it, too, sagged and crumbled in spots. It was replete with the usual nineteenth century industrialist excess of turrets, gables, bay windows, a tower and an elaborate spire, a jumble which spoke of no known architectural school.

We pulled up in front of a cascade of wide, curving steps leading up to a pair of dark, heavy wooden doors banded in black wrought iron which matched the gates. I stepped out and waited for Joy to come around and join me. As she did so, one of the doors opened to reveal a butler, presumably the same man I had spoken to the previous day. I guessed he had been watching the driveway, expecting us to be on time as promised. He was a short man, shorter than me, but stocky, and bald on top except for a few dark threads of hair combed all the way from his left ear over to his right. The attempt to conceal his baldness was only fooling himself.

"Miss Dorothy Stone for Miss Townsend," I announced in my bookstore voice. He nodded, gestured for me to enter, and addressed Joy in the same English accent I had heard on the phone. I had no idea why the Hollywood rich were so obsessed with English butlers, but I supposed it was good news for anybody English and out of work, or at the very least anybody who could do the accent convincingly. More convincingly than Grayson, at least. There was more than one way to make a living as an actor in Los Angeles.

"Driver, are you going to wait for Miss Stone?" he asked Joy.

"Uh, I guess so," she replied, taken aback.

"Then please park your car in the motor court around the side, and wait there until you are called for," he replied.

"I guess I'm not coming inside dressed like this," Joy whispered in my ear and giggled. I tried to keep a straight face. She returned to the hack and I went inside.

I followed the butler into a large foyer which fed, in turn, into a broad corridor. The floor was marble laid out in a repeating geometric mosaic of no great distinction. The walls were wood paneled to the ceiling, oak, I guessed, or something cheaper stained to look like it, with elaborate moldings everywhere.

Despite the lighting, the interior still managed to feel dark and oppressive. Every few feet there hung random Victorian paintings: hunting parties and bucolic English landscapes and moralistic Biblical scenes and portraits which were either miserable relatives of the present owner or more likely a job lot bought at somebody else's estate sale and hung here for the look of the thing. They say money can't buy happiness, but it's supposed to be able to buy interior decor. No wonder Townsend wanted rid of the place. She would do well to throw in the paintings with the house.

We arrived at a door which was incongruously painted eggshell white. The butler knocked, and presumably in response to a reply he heard and I didn't, opened the door and introduced me.

"Miss Stone, to discuss the library, ma'am".

"Thank you, Simmons," she replied, and he withdrew. She was sat at a heavy desk made of rich, dark oak with a green leather inset top, her back turned to me. She continued writing and I took the opportunity to size up the library. The room was larger than my apartment but smaller than Carnegie Hall. Bookshelves on three walls rose to the ceiling, although many of the upper shelves, accessible by sliding ladders, were empty. The lower shelves held various darkly-bound volumes with gilt lettering and decoration on their spines. Many of them were obviously complete sets of the world's so-called classics; exactly the kind of overpriced junk Hooke's store used to specialize in selling to people with little taste and lots of money. Mind you, none of what I could see was particularly rare or especially collectible; even Hooke might have turned his nose up at some them. I would have bet a week's takings most of them were unread.

The fourth wall of the room held the desk where Townsend sat as well as a couple more portraits of somebody's ancestors. She finished whatever she was writing, blotted it, rose, and turned to offer me her hand.

She was dressed in what I believed were called lounging pajamas, raw silk by the look of them, and slippers. I envied her the lifestyle that allowed one to get up in the morning and change out of sleeping pajamas and into lounging pajamas. She was undoubtedly beautiful in the way the daughters of the rich so often are, a product of good breeding, good nutrition, and good hairdressers. She had fine facial features with high cheekbones and a long, narrow nose which did not detract from her looks. Her hair was shoulder length, dark, lightly waved, and looked soft enough to sleep on.

I estimated her to be in her late twenties, although it was harder to tell with the rich. She was about my height. My build, too. We could probably have exchanged clothes if I owned anything she would remotely consider wearing. The only thing our wardrobes had in common was our dress size.

"Please call me Ginnie," she said. "And you're Dorothy, yes?"

"'Dot' is better," I replied. "I don't really like 'Dorothy'."

"Wizard of Oz?" Virginia asked, and I nodded. It was an unexpected note of empathy. "Let's sit down." She led me over to a pair of oversized and overstuffed high-backed green leather library chairs.

I sat on the edge of mine for fear if I sat back, I would need help getting out again. There were so many studs holding the leather to the frame, I wondered if somebody were afraid of the hide coming back to life and taking its revenge on the chair's occupant. Between the chairs was a vaguely Chinese styled, inlaid occasional table, and by her side, a drinks cart.

She picked up a square cut-crystal decanter and poured herself an inch or so into a matching glass. "Something to drink?" she asked me. "Or is it too early for you?"

"Not the first time I've had a drink for breakfast this week," I replied sardonically. "Rye, please, no ice."

"Sorry. Scotch okay?"

"Sure," I said. Maybe it was time to broaden my palate. She handed me a glass. I took a sip and liked it well enough, just not as much as rye.

Ginnie looked me over, I guessed pricing up my outfit, which was the best I had, and rattled her ice noisily. She took a sip of her own Scotch before speaking. "So you've had a quick look. What do you think? Would some of my father's collection do well in your shop?" she asked.

For some reason, I got the sense there was a trap here. I stalled for time. "First, let me offer my condolences for your father's death. I'm sure it's difficult parting with his things."

"Thank you," she said. "But letting go of the estate will be easy. Most of it is junk my grandfather overpaid for, and none of it is to my taste. So, do you think you can take the books off my hands? Outright purchase or consignment?"

It was time to call my own bluff before she called it for me. "In all honesty, I'm really not here about the books."

"I know," she replied. "After your call yesterday, I had my chauffeur drive by your shop. It was immediately obvious this wasn't your stock-in-trade. I was hoping to stretch the game out a little longer, though. By the way, your contempt for this rubbish--" She gestured at the shelves. "--is written all over your face."

"So why didn't you cancel our meeting?" I asked, perplexed.

"Because I'm bloody bored," she replied. "I'm stuck here in this ridiculously huge place sorting out repairs and furniture sales and mortgages and liens by tradesmen my father neglected to pay before his timely death."

I didn't comment on that; there was nothing in it for me.

"Did you know we have a conservatory?" she asked. "Father collected rare orchids, some of them so rare the county tells me it's illegal for me to own them. But it's even more illegal to kill the bloody things, so I have to keep them alive until the Balboa Park arboretum can make arrangements to come up and collect them. Apparently, they are very keen but not very quick."

She took a long pull of her whisky, ice clinking gently against her perfect teeth. I took a sip of my own and kept quiet. This was not something I wanted to interrupt.

"And even when I'm not dealing with tedious nonsense, I'm still quite bored. It turns out most of our so-called family friends were actually my father's friends, and with him gone, they see little reason to include me in their social gatherings. Which is fine by me, they are all thirty or forty years too old. Their daughters my age don't like me much, either. They all think I'm going to flirt with their husbands. I'm not, by the way. They're a loose fraternity of East Coast-educated boys with old money and weak chins, apart from the ones who married into money. They are even worse. And the men like me even less; they all think my imagined roaring single life sets a bad example which will tempt their wives away from quiet domesticity and the rearing of heirs and spares." She finished her drink and immediately poured herself another one.

She had apparently run out of steam for a moment, and I plunged in. "And am I this morning's entertainment, then?" I asked, rather more archly than I'd intended.

"Indeed you are, my dear!" replied Ginnie with no hesitation, topping up my glass unbidden. I suspected she'd started drinking before I had arrived. "My plan was to amuse myself figuring out what your real intentions were. My first thought was casing the place - is that the right word, 'casing'?

- for a burglary. You should know, there is almost nothing here worth stealing, certainly nothing that could be carried out by fewer than three strong men. The candlesticks are silver plate, and the valuable jewelry is in a safety deposit box at the bank. What's here is trinkets and costume jewelry."

I took a quick inventory of her earrings and the rings on her fingers and realized she and I were operating on entirely different scales of 'trinkets'. "I'm happy to deny it's a burglary," I offered. I desperately wanted to tell her the real reason for my visit, but I sensed she needed to get this all out before we could move on.

"Oh, good," she said. "Because that would be such a damn bore. My second guess was some sort of confidence trick, the kind where you persuade me to invest in something that's a guaranteed winner but just shady enough I shouldn't tell anybody about it. And then just when the payoff is supposed to be delivered, you disappear with the money. Is that it?"

"Not that, either," I replied. I was starting to feel it was going to be quite awkward when she finally allowed me to speak my piece.

"My last guess was you're a medium with some predictions vital to my safety to sell me. I have to tell you, that would be my least favorite answer. I don't have any patience for such nonsense."

I shook my head.

"Well then, I'm all out of ideas. You will have to tell me." And with that, she settled back into her chair, cradling her drink in both hands.

"It's about Mr. Dalton," I said. "I have fears for his safety."

Her mood changed immediately. She sat forward and stiffly upright. She banged her glass down on the table, the ice cubes bouncing almost free of the glass. All traces of amusement disappeared from her face. "I have no desire to discuss whatever mess Mr. Dalton has gotten himself into. He and I are not on speaking terms, and I have no wish to change that."

"But--" I started.

"This conversation is over," she said coldly and firmly. "You should leave now." She reached under the table and, I assume, pressed a buzzer. Simmons must have been waiting right outside because he appeared instantly.

"Show Miss Stone to her car immediately," said Townsend curtly. Simmons nodded and held the door open for me. Too stunned to do anything else, I meekly got up and walked out the door, before following him along a short passage and through a side door opening onto the motor court. The court was simply an open graveled area bounded on one side by the house, on a second by a carriage house large enough to house four cars, on the third by the driveway leading around to the front of the house, and on the fourth by open parkland which fell away to a small lake.

A limo was parked in the court, a black Lincoln Continental polished to a high shine, a 1942 from shortly before all the car makers switched over to wartime production. It was beautiful, but not as beautiful as the young man leaning casually against it and chatting with Joy. He had the looks of a Valentino: dark, enigmatic, and sleek as an

Arabian thoroughbred. Like a lot of waiters, chauffeurs, valet parkers, and bell boys in this town, he was just doing his time until he was spotted by a producer and could embark on his true calling as a matinee idol.

Joy broke off their conversation when she saw me. She waved to me, said her goodbyes to him, and joined me at her cab. The matinee idol-in-waiting turned away and resumed pretending to polish the already blemish-free Lincoln. I slipped sullenly into my seat. We sat in silence for ten minutes as Joy steered us back towards my shop.

Finally, Joy spoke up. "I'm guessing it didn't go well, the way you got eighty-sixed out the side door?" she said.

"It did not go well at all. Townsend is one of the bored and idle rich in the worst way, and she lost interest the moment I stopped being entertaining. Which, by coincidence, is the moment I brought up Dalton." On top of everything else, I was resenting the time I had spent anxiously plotting a strategy to get in the front door, only to get thrown out the side so promptly.

"How did she take it?" asked Joy.

"Very badly indeed," I replied. "She completely shut me down and made it clear they were on the outs."

"Well, if it makes you feel any better, I got a ton of gossip out of Toby."

"The cute chauffeur? Did you get a date with him?" I asked. I wasn't in the best of moods, and Joy's success to my failure wasn't helping.

"If I had, I'd be the first girl who did," Joy laughed.

I had to think about that for a few seconds. Then the penny dropped. "Then how did you get him to open up?" I thought domestic staff were supposed to be discreet if they wanted to keep their positions.

"Easy. He hinted he had some juicy gossip, one driver to another, and I pretended I wasn't interested. After that, he couldn't tell me enough about all the goings on."

"Clever," I said. "Did you get that trick from Dalton, or cheap detective stories?"

"Neither," smirked Joy. "Sherlock Holmes. Your favorite detective."

Holmes did nothing to improve my mood, but I set him aside. "Okay, smarty. What did you get?"

"It turns out Dalton was seeing her a lot, maybe two or three times a week. Matches what you saw in the diary. Some nights they went out, her always much better dressed than him. Toby was pretty rude about Dalton's clothes, which was funny for a guy who wears a badly-fitting uniform to work. Other nights, they stayed in and Toby got the night off. As far as he could tell, those nights, they sat in the parlor and both drank while she read and he ferreted away at the notebook. Sometimes, he'd stay over, other times he got a late cab home.

"Anyway, the last time he was here, it was unusual because it was mid-afternoon. And they had a blazing row Toby could hear through the windows. He couldn't make out everything, but the gist of it was Dalton was complaining about money, and she wanted him to quit anyway because she had more than enough money for both of them. It ended with her throwing a glass at the floor and him storming out, slamming doors behind him. He marched straight to the motor court, and Toby had to jump to not be caught listening. He got in the back of the cab, slammed that door, too, and it drove away. He hasn't been back since."

"Wow. When was this?"

"About two weeks ago, the day before his no-show for my pickup."

The story sounded very dramatic. Something else had started bothering me too, but I didn't want to say it out loud in front of Joy. Why was Dalton spending so much time on the book? Why hadn't he just thrown it in one of Townsend's many fireplaces? Could that also be what they were arguing about? Not much was making sense today, and my mood became as sour as milk left out in the sun.

Chapter Ten

Joy dropped me back at the shop, with no sightings of a black Nash along the way. There was, however, an absolutely stunning pre-war red Cadillac Sixty Special, a '41 I thought, parked about twenty feet from my door. It would have drawn stares even parked on the expensive side of the boulevard. I was pretty sure the owner wasn't shopping for supplies at George's hardware store. As I opened up the store, I saw the driver's door open and a tall, slim man slid out. He was wearing a crisply pressed black chauffeur's uniform, complete with cap and white gloves.

I stepped inside, closed the door behind me, and watched from the window as he opened the rear door. Out stepped a solidly-built man in a charcoal gray double-breasted, pin-striped suit, buttoned high on the chest, a style that had been fashionable back when the Caddy was new. He waited patiently as the chauffeur reached inside, pulled out a three-quarter length camelhair coat, and draped it over his shoulders like a cloak before going back for a brown Fedora. He was dressed for Chicago's winter, not LA's. Fully attired now, he walked over to my store, leaving the driver to watch the car.

The sign on my door said 'Closed', but somehow, it didn't stop him from coming in. I would have to see if George could fix that.

He closed the door behind himself and turned the lock. He moved to the center of the room, crowding me towards the back. He seemed to take up more space than physically possible; words like "over-bearing" and "intimidating" scrolled across my inner thesaurus. He propped his hat on top of one of the book stacks. I really had to get a hat stand, I thought. His hair was jet black, thinning and slicked back. His face was hard, his age hard to guess. Maybe fifty, but I wouldn't bet money on it.

"My name is Accardo," he announced. "Mr. Grayson might have mentioned me."

It explained the suit. I guessed the prison guards had taken it off him when he went inside and given it back when he came out. "If you're after protection money, I'm afraid you've come to the wrong store," I replied, projecting far more confidence than I felt. "I can barely make rent. The best I can offer you is payment-in-kind in used paperbacks, if you read much. You'd probably do better across the street, although not at Hooke's, what with him still being dead."

It was sheer bravado on my part. For all I knew, Accardo was the one who'd had Hooke killed. He glared at me and said nothing, so I continued burying myself. "On the other hand, if you're going to burn the place down, could you give me a couple of weeks to re-up my insurance? I could even over-insure it and then we could split the profits. What do you think?"

Sometimes, my eyes tried to look at my own mouth because they couldn't believe the stupid things coming out of it. This was one of those times.

Accardo stared, his face betraying no reaction. The clock ticked off a few seconds. "Are you like this with all your customers?" he finally asked.

"Not at all," I replied. "The sarcasm is complimentary only for special visitors who come in here to intimidate me and leave without buying anything."

"Maybe I'm a customer, but only for one very specific book," he said.

"1865 Vanity Fair?" I offered. He looked every bit as perplexed as Grayson had. I made a mental note to ask Joy why the book mattered.

"A certain black leather notebook. You know what's in it."

I had a pretty good idea.

"I know Grayson offered you a few hundred. I will pay you a thousand dollars, no questions asked about how you get hold of it."

"And what if I don't want to sell it to you?" I asked. I did not like the thought of the book in Accardo's hands. Some of the people in there might be as bad as he was, but others were merely weasels like Grayson. And I wasn't sure anybody deserved to be blackmailed, regardless of what they'd done. If some of them were politicians, it could be very bad.

Accardo took a step closer to me. "This isn't a request, Miss Stone," he said, a certain edge in his voice. "You're going to find the book for me, I'm going to give you a grand, and we'll be done with each other's business. Understand?"

"Out of interest, what will you do with the book?" I sounded a lot steadier than I felt. This was not a man I could tease like I had Grayson.

"I'm going to destroy it."

I raised both eyebrows.

"Several valuable business associates of mine appear in it. Politicians, actors, other public figures. I will see that no harm comes to them, and in return, they will each owe me a favor. I'm sure Grayson told you I wanted to restart the blackmail racket, but that's his kind of business, not mine."

I reflected that an awful lot of people were going to an awful lot of trouble over a book none of them supposedly wanted to exploit. "He told me he only wanted his own page," I said.

"It was generous of you to believe him," Accardo responded. "He's into some pretty shady stuff."

"I didn't think he was up to anything worse than an illegal casino, bribing the local law enforcement, and some minor tax evasion."

"They put Capone away for tax evasion. Did he tell you about the girls?"

I chewed on Accardo's words for a few moments. I didn't want to know about the girls, but apparently Grayson had played me at least as much as I had played him. I wondered what else he had lied about. How naive had I been? Finally: "If I had the book - and let me be clear, I don't - I would want two more things in return for it." I knew I didn't have much of a negotiating position, but I had to ask.

"Try me," said Accardo.

"First, call off your tail. The black Nash." I assumed it had to be Accardo's, if Grayson had, in fact, kept his promise. "That one's really just a courtesy. We've already proven we can lose it any time we choose."

"And the second?"

"The safe return of Dalton." There it was, out in the open. Accusation and demand all in one.

"The first, consider it done. A courtesy between business partners, as you say. The second is going to be a lot harder."

"Why?" I asked, but my brain instantly knew the answer.

"Dalton has been dead for more than a week. Grayson killed him."

I stepped back, bumping into my own desk and tottered forward again. I barely knew Dalton, but this thought, that somebody I had met had been murdered, I didn't know where to put it. I barely knew the man, yet the news delivered so abruptly was still shocking. "That doesn't make sense. Grayson wants the book found, too. Why would he kill Dalton?"

"He screwed up," shrugged Accardo, and grabbed his coat at the shoulders to save it from falling to the floor. "His men were trying to beat it out of Dalton and they overdid it. Amateurs." He seemed more upset by this last than Dalton's death. I was still trying to file the facts in the right order. "Anyway, that's why he came to you. Right now, you look like his best lead on the book."

My brain was buzzing, trying to find a new scenario to fit all the pieces together. "How could you possibly know all this?" I demanded.

Accardo shrugged again, a little more cautiously this time. "Same way I know he offered you money. I have a guy inside his operation. So I figured, time for somebody with a more business-like approach to step in before he hurts anybody else."

All the puzzle pieces I thought I had cleverly slotted into place were now upside down. This was the trouble with incomplete puzzles: sometimes, the pieces could go together to make more than one picture.

And Dalton was dead. We had been chasing a ghost this whole time.

"I can see you've got a lot to think about," Accardo said. "Call me when you have something for me." He took a business card out of his breast pocket and snapped it down on the table. "Otherwise, I'll have somebody check in with you after the weekend." And with that, he placed his hat back on his head, adjusted it to his satisfaction, turned on the heel of his highly-polished brogues, and left.

The room suddenly felt a lot bigger without him in it. I locked the door behind him and watched through the window as the chauffeur reversed his earlier ritual. He opened the rear door, took the hat and coat, handed them in behind Accardo, and closed the door before taking his own place behind the wheel. The red Caddy eased away from the curb, turning heads with all the indifference of a swan on a perfectly still lake. I picked up his card. It read, Michael Accardo, and on the next line, Hospitality Supplies and Services, and finally a phone number.

I had no idea how I was going to break the news to Joy.

Or, for that matter, Townsend.

Once he was gone and I had regained my equilibrium, I called and left a message for Joy with Madge. I was pretty sure she'd be at Jack's bar by evening, but I wanted to be sure I wouldn't miss her. I'd thought about asking her to come to the store, but I figured she'd probably need a drink when she heard the news; and more familiar surroundings were probably better, too.

I arrived at the bar around six, and my rye was in Jack's hand before the door closed behind me. I'd never been a regular at a bar before, and it felt nice in an odd kind of way. I was confident it was more to do with Joy's stamp of approval than anything I had done. I was even starting to get used to the smells of spilled drinks and other people's cigarettes.

The usual clutch of drivers were at their table and I joined them, squeezing in next to Madge where I could watch the door for Joy's arrival. I didn't see Mikey, and asked after him. One of the other drivers told me he was back at the garage working on a couple of the cars. He often didn't get to the bar until after seven, apparently.

I sipped my rye as slowly as I could manage - I wanted a clear head for what was coming next - and after ten minutes or so, Joy arrived. I excused myself from the table and went over to meet her. I steered her, beer in hand, to a small table well away from the other drivers.

She got her Lucky going and looked across at me. "It's bad news, isn't it?" she said.

"How can you tell?" I replied.

"The table to ourselves. Plus you look terrible."

"Right. I've spent the afternoon trying to find a gentle way to say this. It's about Dalton."

"He's dead," said Joy flatly.

I nodded. I was deeply surprised at the lack of reaction from her, but also hugely relieved to have it out so readily. "I'm afraid so." I tried to be equally flat.

"You'd better give me the details," she sighed. I told her all about Accardo's visit and his bombshell revelation.

"Do you believe him?" she asked when I was done.

"About Dalton being dead, yes. I don't see why he'd lie. He wants us to find the book, and this gives us less incentive, not more. As far as the rest goes, I'm not so sure." As I listened to myself saying this, a part of my brain was screaming at the rest to not be so darn analytical and try empathizing a bit more.

"Why would he put Grayson in the frame?" asked Joy, puzzled.

"He wants the book, and he knows Grayson wants it, too. It's in his interest for us to think Grayson is the bad guy here. Or worse guy, I guess. Neither of them are exactly saints."

"Yeah, that tracks," replied Joy. She seemed down, but not nearly the reaction I'd been expecting.

"Are you okay?" I asked.

"It's… confusing. I mean, I liked Dalton well enough, and it's a shock and all. But really, I only knew him for three months, and in all that time, he was strictly business. I don't think he ever once asked me how I was doing, or what I did outside work. So I'm sad, but I'm not, you know, wailing and tearing my clothes sad. I lost a good customer, not a good friend."

"Still… I worried this would hit you harder."

"To be honest, I'd already thought he might be dead. It's been two weeks. If somebody had kidnapped him to make him talk, how long are they going to keep around a guy who isn't going to spill?"

Something still seemed missing, even to my limited social skills, and I said so.

Joy looked up from her drink and held my gaze for several seconds. "You're right, there is something else. It's about time I told you the story."

"I think we should have fresh drinks for this," I said. Joy nodded her agreement.

With our refilled glasses in front of us and newly lit cigarettes in hand, Joy took a deep breath and jumped in. "So. I flew bombers during the war."

"What? How? I didn't think they let women fly," I interrupted.

"Not combat, sure," she explained. "Transport. There were a bunch of us, a thousand or so, who flew planes from the factories to the east coast for shipping, or to bases for training. I flew B-17s out of a Boeing factory in Seattle. They weren't sure we could handle the bombers, but they needed the men for combat, so they gave us a shot and we proved them wrong.

"What came next were the best years of my life. Flying a big plane like that is like standing on the high diving board. Driving a cab is like paddling around in the kiddie pool in comparison. And I had the best bunch of girls to work with, too."

I nodded. I felt the same way about my wartime work and made a mental bookmark to share my story with Joy sometime soon. Not now.

"Great parties, too, any time we delivered to a training base," she continued. "Supposedly there was no fraternization, but everybody on base looked the other way. We all knew how dangerous flying bombers over Europe was, and nobody wanted to tell those boys they couldn't have one last fling Stateside before shipping out."

I nodded, sipped my rye, lit another Kool.

"But it wasn't the safest job ever," she went on. "Those were pretty crude machines, built as fast and as cheap as they could churn them out. And remember, we were the first people to fly these planes, straight off the factory floor. If there was anything wrong, we were the crew who would find out." Her face got dark. She stared down at her beer. One tear escaped the inside corner of her left eye and made its slow track down the side of her nose.

"So this was '43. June. Perfect flying weather, just a regular delivery run to an airfield in the Midwest. My crew and another were bringing our B-17s in on parallel runways. My friend Maria was navigator on the other plane. I say 'friend' but I have to tell you about Maria. Some people have a childhood friend, a best friend in school, or a big sister. She was all that to me, rolled into one person, even though I'd only known her a few months. We met on the first day of training and after that we were together every chance we got. And if you think I'm upbeat, you should have met Maria. She could light up any room she was in.

"Anyway, the flight had been completely routine, clear weather and great visibility the whole way. Our touchdown was perfect, and as soon as I had us rolling to a stop, I looked across to the other plane. I saw it was nose-down and skewing sideways. The port landing gear had collapsed on landing and the nose had plowed into the ground. The navigator seat in those B-17s is right up front and on the port side, a really bad place to be in a crash like that.

"As soon as I got the plane stopped, we jumped out and ran over, but it was way too late. She was squeezed tight between two struts, not breathing. The weirdest part was she looked fine, like she was sleeping. The doc said crush injuries could be like that, but she probably died very quickly after impact. The rest of the crew got out with just bumps and bruises."

Joy looked up and met my eyes again. She'd been quietly crying the whole time she was telling that part of the story. She wiped her face with the palm of her hand.

I tried to think of something to say that wasn't completely stupid. "God, I'm sorry," I said. It was painfully inadequate. Something struck me. "That flight jacket you wear. It's not yours, is it? It's hers," I said.

Joy nodded.

"Is that when you quit flying?" I asked.

Joy shook her head. "I wanted to keep going, and I did, for another year and a half. But they shuttered the program at the end of '44. They had more flight instructors than they could use, so they gave them our jobs. And with all those hero flyboys coming home, no airline was going to give a pilot's job to a woman. So I started driving a cab. But honestly, I feel like they're going to push me out of that, too, and give my drive to a vet."

"Damn," I said, which was pretty much the strongest language I had ever used out loud. "Two years ago, they were telling us 'You can do it!' and 'Go rivet that battleship'. Now it's 'stay home and bake cakes'." I felt sad, angry, and sick all at the same time.

"Anyway," continued Joy. "After I lost Maria, I…well, I just sort of skated by. I chatted with friends, went on dates, drank more than I should, but I wasn't really feeling it. No great lows, no great highs, just… flat. Even when I seemed upbeat, I felt distanced from it, you know? Like I was watching a good time, not having a good time."

I knew exactly what she meant.

"So I wasn't really committed to anything. Or anybody," she continued. "And ever since, I really haven't let anybody get close to me. Until you, kiddo." She smiled as best she could, considering the circumstances.

"You told me a few days back you had trouble keeping a boyfriend. Is this what you were referring to?" I asked.

"Uh huh. My last boyfriend told me I was too much hard work, that it was tough being with somebody who was so self-reliant all the time. He said he wanted somebody who needed him at least once in a while." She sighed and shrugged, wiped her face again. "I guess these days I'm just a better date than girlfriend."

I reached across the table and took her hand. "And a better friend than either."

She got up, came around the table to me, and gave me a hug for much longer than I was truly comfortable with. I couldn't help suspecting it was partly to hide the fact that she was crying again.

Finally, she sat back down. "Thank you," she said.

"Is it appropriate to drink a toast in memory of Maria?" I asked.

"It certainly is," Joy replied.

And we did.

Chapter Eleven

I didn't see Joy again until Monday. She said she needed a couple of days getting back to her regular life, just picking up and dropping off fares and swapping banter with her fellow drivers. No mysteries, no missing notebooks, no threats from gangsters. I had no objections. Even though she hadn't seemed to take the news about Dalton too hard at the time, these things can sometimes take a couple of days to sink in, I knew, and she might well need some time alone to reflect and digest. I was confident Madge and the other drivers would take good care of her if necessary, probably better care than I could.

As for myself, my thoughts were uncharacteristically muddled. I wasn't even sure I still cared about finding the book. Maybe this whole interlude was over and I should go back to my regular life of selling books and worrying about money. I'd probably lost a quarter of my business this past week on this fool's errand. That would have gone a long way to paying my rent. With Dalton reportedly dead - and the more I thought about it, the more I believed it - any sense of urgency was certainly gone.

I'd originally gotten sucked into the whole business because I was mad about the break-in, and then stayed out of concern for Dalton when I didn't even know what the book contained. And if I was honest with myself, because it was a lot more exciting than being a down-at-heel used bookseller. Now the only thing at stake was whether the book fell into the hands of somebody who would use it for blackmail. Of course, it was easy for me to say "only" when my name wasn't in there.

But if I continued to chase the book, was I making it worse or better? If I didn't find it, Accardo or Grayson probably would, eventually. And if I did find it first, I would certainly have to hand it over. Accardo had made that clear. But so what if I did? I didn't for a moment believe either Accardo's or Grayson's assurances that they weren't going to restart the blackmail racket, but in any case, it hardly seemed my concern. The only name I knew was in there was Grayson. I didn't much care what happened to him, and anyway, he probably treated light blackmail as a cost of doing business. If he or anybody else in the book cared enough, they would have to go to the cops.

And yet, I still felt uneasy about letting it go. Maybe there were other people in the book who didn't deserve to be blackmailed, and couldn't shrug off the cost like Grayson. And maybe I could do something about it if I found the book first.

Or maybe I could get myself killed crossing Accardo.

Of course, this was assuming both Grayson and Accardo would let me resign my informal commission. Both of them seemed to think I knew far more than I did, and I was their best bet for finding the book since Dalton was dead. It was largely my own fault for bluffing. Whether or not I cared might well be moot.

My thoughts were chasing their own tail and I was no nearer to a resolution, but for now I had to set it aside. I still had something important I had to do. I needed to find a way to let Ginnie Townsend know about Dalton, and it was going to be hard to so much as get a foot in the door. I didn't expect her to even take my call.

The shop was busy all day Saturday, the way it was supposed to be. I tried to call twice on Saturday evening after closing, but nobody was picking up. I guessed Ginnie was out socializing, or whatever it is socialites do, and if I cared to know the details I could check the gossip columns on Monday. Presumably, Simmons had the night off when Ginnie was out late. Or perhaps he didn't and had simply decided there was nothing in it for him in answering the phone.

I waited until a decent hour on Sunday to try again, which by my standards meant after ten. It meant going in to the store. I didn't open on Sundays, but I had a phone line there. The phone was picked up after five rings, and I heard the perfect English accent again. Having met Simmons in person, I now wondered at how deep his voice was. He had the tenor of a much bigger man. I also wondered how long he had been in America, and how he protected his accent from becoming Americanized. Or even if the accent was entirely fake to begin with. Was it something you learned at butler school?

I stopped wondering long enough to say my name and to ask if I might speak to Miss Townsend. Simmons told me to wait, and I heard his footsteps receding. Then silence. And eventually footsteps returning. Simmons picked up the phone again and told me Miss Townsend had informed him she was not at home. She might return my call later, I was told. I filed it under Unlikely. I had done everything I could for now, short of camping on her doorstep, so it was up to her. If nothing happened in a week, I could write her a letter, which I immediately began mentally composing.

I shut down my internal letter writer and took a simple moment to enjoy the store being quiet. It was different on a Sunday, when quiet was what it was supposed to be. When it was empty during opening hours, I was all anxious anticipation, hoping for a customer. I realized to my surprise I also liked the store better when it was full of people. I could flit from customer to customer, conversation to conversation, with always a ready excuse to escape when I felt uncomfortable. But when there were just one or two customers, I felt obliged to engage with them. And so often the conversations would turn personal: "You're so young to be running a bookshop!"; "It must be lovely to have so much freedom!"; "All these books, you're so lucky!".

Sunday at the store was also the only time and place I allowed myself to think about my father. My happiest childhood memories with him were of sitting in the office doing my homework; when other children went to the library to look things up, I went to our bookshelves. After closing, we would walk to a nearby restaurant for dinner, with dessert if it had been a particularly good day. I also loved listening to him in the shop chatting up customers. He seemed to get on with everybody; he just had a genuine liking for people, and they for him. I had not inherited the trait, nor could I even fake it convincingly. Maybe it was why he was able to make the bookshop pay.

I also reflected he would not be running around like this, leaving the store closed at random hours. Worse than the financial losses, if I didn't keep regular hours, people would simply stop coming for fear I would be closed. I understood some time very soon, I needed to make a hard decision: either I had to commit myself to the store or I had to give up. I could not simply sit around for the next three months watching it fade away or waiting to be evicted. I had been avoiding facing the facts for months now, but if I didn't change something, I quite simply was going to run out of money.

The rest of Sunday lay stretched out before me, and I took the opportunity to clear my head of everything related to Hooke, Dalton, a mysterious, missing notebook, and what I might do next; and even of my bookshop worries. Picking up the Jane Austen I'd been trying to read for some days now, I locked the store behind me and took a slow walk down to the park. I sat myself under the same river birch where previously I'd sipped rye with Joy while images of a dead body and a blood-stained carpet had floated across my inner eye.

Today was better. A crisp, cool morning with, for once, no sign of rain later. The park was popular on Sundays. A family sat picnicking under one of the other trees, and a father and son were tossing a baseball back and forth. Other people, mostly couples and families, came and went, full of happy chatter and loving gazes. They didn't bother me, and soon I disappeared into my book.

By the time I returned to the store, it was after three. I had spent a delightful afternoon in the park simply reading, I had finished the Austen, and my mind felt as calm as it had at any point in weeks. As I opened the door, I heard the phone ringing. I rushed to my office and picked up. To my surprise, it was Townsend. Not her butler with a dismissive message to pass on, but the lady herself.

"I wanted to apologize," she said. "I may have been a tiny bit petulant when we met, and quite possibly slightly drunk. Could we perhaps start over?"

"Even though I have no interest in the books?" I asked.

"Yes. I should pay attention to what you have to say about Dalton. Regardless of how badly he and I squabbled, I feel some residual obligation towards him. Can you come by tomorrow morning, say around nine? I promise to be sober."

I readily agreed. As soon as we hung up, I called the dispatcher - it was an unfamiliar voice, not Madge - and asked her to let Joy know I would be needing a ride in the morning.

I took a streetcar home. All the hard-won calm I had earned that afternoon had been dissipated by Townsend's call. This was going to be an unpredictable meeting, and I doubted whether any amount of rehearsal could prepare me for it.

Chapter Twelve

Monday was another routinely bright, clear, perfect morning with rain clouds forming up over the hills, lined up for their scheduled afternoon performance. Joy surprised me when she picked me up. Instead of Maria's flight jacket, she was wearing a black wool car coat.

"I did a lot of thinking over the weekend, and I realized it was time to make some changes," she told me. "You can't mourn the same person forever, you know? I'll always miss Maria, but I also have to live my life. And I have to make room for other people."

We didn't talk about it any further on the way over to Ginnie's house, but the silence didn't feel uncomfortable. It just felt like the right time for quiet. I kept an eye out for the Nash with the dented fender, but didn't spot it. That meant either Accardo had kept his promise or he was tailing us with a different car. If it was the latter, they were doing a better job than either of our two previous tails.

A few minutes before nine, we pulled up in front of the steps of the Townsend pile. Joy let me out and pulled around to the motor court without waiting to be told. Simmons led me inside to what he informed me was the front parlor. I didn't ask how many other parlors there were. This one was a high-ceilinged room, half-paneled in oak, stained rather than painted to show off the quality of the wood, and more of the same paintings that were everywhere else in the house. The parlor jutted out from the rest of the house, and there were tall windows on three sides overlooking the park, the lake, and the motor court. It was easy to see how Toby could have listened in on a loud argument here.

On one wall was a fireplace, a couple of logs burning in it more for effect than for heat, and on the wall opposite, a large tapestry hung almost from ceiling to floor. To the left of the fireplace was a group of four high-backed chairs arranged in an arc around a low table so all of them could see the fire, and on the other side, the arrangement was mirrored. Underneath it all, an elaborate, oriental rug with dragons chasing each other around the perimeter tied the grouping together. Ginnie got up from her chair and walked over to meet me. She noticed my interest in the tapestry.

"It's a fake, you know, and not even a very good one," she said. "My grandfather bought it in Europe and had it shipped here, believing it was 15th century. I can only hope whoever buys this place wants it, because I'm sure I don't know how one disposes of something like this. I expect as I wind this place down, a lot of the other so-called antiques are going to turn out to be equally bogus."

"I'm sorry about that," I said, for want of anything intelligent or useful to offer.

Ginnie waved it off. "It doesn't matter now. If it made him happy to think they were real, he could afford to be swindled just a little bit. What else is rich people's money for? Anyway, come and sit down." She led me over to the left-hand group of chairs. They were a lot more practical than the ones in the library; I didn't feel like I might need help getting out when the time came.

On the table in front of us, a tea service was set out. There was no drinks cart in sight. Ginnie poured tea for us both without asking if I wanted one and told me to help myself to milk and sugar. I didn't really drink tea, but I didn't want to complain, and I figured if I put enough milk and sugar in it, I wouldn't taste the tea.

"I have to say, this feels a bit uncomfortable after last week. This seems like a big turnaround," I offered.

"Let me apologize for Friday, and try to explain," Ginnie replied. "On Thursday night, I was angry about John - Dalton, that is - and I'd been drinking. I was sure he'd come crawling back with flowers and apologies after a couple of days, so when he still hadn't shown up a week later, I drank too much. I woke up on Friday with a rotten hangover and started drinking again right away."

"I rather guessed you might have been a couple of drinks ahead of me," I said tentatively.

"Anyway, thank you for keeping me company at that time of the morning. You did surprise me."

"It's a recent habit," I said. "And not one I'm proud of. So I'm glad we're starting the day with tea this time."

"Anyway, I took my anger at John out on you, and I'm sorry for that. I'm still angry at him, but I am also concerned. Last time you were here, you said John was in trouble. You'd better tell me what's going on."

I took a large gulp of tea and steeled myself. "I'm afraid it's worse than trouble. A man came to my store on Friday and told me Dalton is dead. We believe him. I'm very sorry."

Ginnie nodded a couple of times, staring at the empty fireplace, took some tea, and put her cup down on the table extremely carefully. I thought there might have been just the slightest tremble. "Thank you for reaching out and letting me know. I'm sure that can't have been easy, especially after the way I treated you before." I supposed a certain amount of sang-froid was taught at the better schools.

"I'm glad I was able to tell you in person. It's not the sort of news one should hear by telephone. Are you okay?"

"I'm more upset than I'm going to let you see, if that's what you're asking. That's how I was raised. But I'm not as upset as you are probably imagining, which is also how I was raised. Anyway, tell me more about this mysterious visitor. What exactly did he say?"

"It's a long story and a bit complicated," I replied. I was deeply unsure how much detail I should share.

"Then you'd better start at the beginning. Wait, you said 'we' earlier?"

"Yes, my friend Joy and I. She knows more about this than I do."

"But she couldn't be with you today?"

"Oh, she's here, waiting with the car in your motor court. She's a taxi driver by trade, and she drove us here. Simmons didn't seem to think she should come in the house."

Ginnie leant forward and picked up a charming little porcelain bell that matched the teapot and cups and gave it a gentle shake. A few moments passed, and Simmons appeared at her side.

"Simmons, would you please bring in Miss Stone's driver?" she asked. "Thank you."

Once Simmons was gone, I started my story. "From the very beginning then. I only met Dalton once, and briefly," I said. I explained how he had come to my store, asking about the book. "By the way, do you know why he wanted an 1865

Vanity Fair? I'm sure it has something to do with the Hooke case, but I have no idea what."

"I don't have any more idea than you, I'm afraid," she replied. "I bought one for him, and it's still around here somewhere. John insisted it had to be that particular edition. You're welcome to borrow it, if you think it will help."

At that moment, Simmons escorted Joy into the room. He didn't look happy about it. Joy took the seat next to me, and Ginnie poured tea for her. Joy looked even less pleased about that than I had. Ginnie asked Joy how she had known Dalton and Joy gave her the same explanation she had given me from what seemed like a lifetime ago, but in reality, was only a week. Ginnie nodded along.

"We were just talking about the Vanity Fair," I said. "And I realized I never asked you if you knew what it was about." I turned to Ginnie. "It was actually the book that first led Joy to me."

"Oh, sure," said Joy. "Dalton told me. I didn't say anything about it before because it didn't seem like a big deal. Basically, he saw the book on Hooke's desk when he was in his store posing as a customer. He said it looked out of place because it was in pretty poor condition, very different from everything else in the shop. He'd reached for it, and the girl who worked there had slapped his hand away, telling him not to touch because it was an 1865. He said he must have looked blank because she added, "first American edition". Then she put the book away in a desk drawer and locked it. He left and set about trying to find a copy for himself because the whole episode bothered him. It was out of place, in his words. As far as I know, he never did find one, and he never did figure out what it had to do with anything, either. And that's all."

I didn't feel much wiser. Maybe the book mattered, maybe it was just a sentimental liking of Hooke's. Perhaps he had better taste in books than the people he sold to. Did everything have to mean something? But I felt like I was still missing a piece, or probably more than one. I parked it in the part of my brain which works on problems when I'm thinking about something else.

Setting that aside, I started explaining to Ginnie what Joy and I had been up to. I left out some disturbing details - she didn't need to know about the dead body in Dalton's office or the man with a gun in his apartment - and Joy jumped in when I missed anything. Ginnie took it all in silently and patiently until I mentioned Grayson coming to my store. Then she interrupted.

"Wait, you know Anthony Grayson?"

"Only enough to know he's mixed up in this business somehow. How do you know him?"

"I throw money away at his casino," said Ginnie. "Besides playing the horses, I also like to play the tables. Obviously, it's not legal, but it's harmless enough, in my opinion."

She went to pour herself another cup of tea and discovered the pot was empty. She summoned Simmons again, handed him the pot and sent him off in search of fresh tea. He looked even less happy about this errand.

I finished with the tale of Accardo's visit to my store. When I got to his accusation against Grayson, I shared my doubts about Accardo's veracity. Ginnie echoed those doubts.

"Grayson is certainly crooked, but that doesn't sound like him at all," she said.

"Now you know as much as we do," I finally said. It wasn't completely true, but true enough for now.

She sat slowly back in her chair, her empty teacup balanced on her lap, looking thoughtful.

"You're taking this remarkably well," I offered. I was beginning to wonder whether anybody really missed Dalton.

"I suppose I am," replied Ginnie. "You have to understand, I was never under any illusion that John was the love of my life. We had fun going out together, but it was not what you would call a romance. He got a kick out of my rich friends and my social events. I got a thrill out of being with a private detective, and frankly I enjoyed watching his bad manners upset my friends. But we argued all the time almost from the off, mostly about money. I knew it wasn't going to last, and that fairly quickly one of us would get bored with the other. Or with the arguing."

Something else struck me. "Did he have family? Other friends I should let know about his passing?"

"If he did, he never mentioned them to me," replied Ginnie, ruefully. "In fact, he didn't talk at all about the rest of his personal life. And for all I know, I was just one of a whole slate of girlfriends, his Tuesday-and-Thursday girl." If she was, his diary didn't show it, I thought to myself. But it didn't seem worth getting into right now. I was more bemused by the fact that Dalton was such a complete blank slate to both Joy and Ginnie.

I dragged my mind back to the business at hand. "I understand you argued the afternoon before he disappeared?" I didn't tell her how I knew, and hoped she wouldn't ask.

"Yes, it was our usual argument," she replied. "It always went the same way. We would come back from a party or wherever, and he would complain that my friends looked down on him, that he would never fit in, his clothes looked too shabby, he didn't have an expensive watch or cufflinks, and so on. Then I would offer to take him shopping because I had money enough for both of us. Then he would say he didn't want my money, but it was impossible to make a decent living as an honest private eye in this town." She paused.

"After that, we would always have a drink and then sit, ignoring each other until either he went home or we went to bed. I would read and he would fiddle about with that stupid notebook of his." Both Joy and I nodded along to all this. She continued.

"But that afternoon - we had got back from the races and his cab had just arrived to take him home - I took it one step further. One step too far, it turned out. I told him that if he couldn't make ends meet as an honest detective, maybe he should try being a dishonest one. Then we both yelled a bit, I threw a glass, and he stormed out. That was the last time I saw or heard from him. Now I wish we'd parted on a better note," she finished sadly.

We all sat and brooded on that for a moment.

"What will you two do now?" asked Ginnie. "If John is truly dead, it sounds like this is over for both of you."

Joy and I looked at each other. I realized we hadn't talked about it.

"I can't speak for Joy, but I don't think I'm done," I said, speaking first. "For one, I want to know for sure who killed Dalton. Of the three of us, I knew him the least, but it doesn't seem right to just let it go. And I can't take what I know to the police without getting Joy and myself tangled up in it all. I don't know much about the law, but we're probably guilty of all kinds of things if the police want to make it that way."

Ginnie nodded. "More likely, they won't even take you seriously. Without a body, they'll treat it as a missing persons case. Which is to say, do nothing." We both looked at her; I think Joy had the same question on her mind that I did. She picked up on it before either of us asked.

"Oh. Dalton talked a lot about old cases, and I absorbed a thing or two," Ginnie said. "He didn't hold our city police department in very high regard."

I reflected that he wasn't the only one. "There's also the book," I said. "We think it's a ledger of Hooke's blackmail victims, probably a way of keeping his pornography customers in line, as well as an extra source of income. It seems wrong to leave it just floating around out there."

"That's what Dalton suspected, too," said Ginnie. That left me confused.

"Suspected? How could he not know?" I asked.

"Oh, I though you knew this. The book is mostly in code."

"Mostly?" said Joy. This was not getting any clearer.

"Yes, John showed it to me once. Each page has a victim's last name at the top in plain language, then several lines of numbers in groups, and finally some dates and numbers in plain text. Presumably payments," said Ginnie.

I chewed on that. "That makes more sense. All that time he spent with it..." I said.

"He was trying to crack the code?" asked Joy.

I nodded.

"That's right," said Ginnie. "As I said, he spent a lot of evenings here working on it. He said he wasn't getting anywhere, though."

"There's another thing bugging me," I said. "If it came from the Hooke investigation, shouldn't he have turned it over to the police?"

"I can explain that," said Ginnie. "He didn't trust them to keep it confidential. Somebody would surely sell the juiciest names to the gossip columnists, and worse if they managed to decode it. The DA's office is better, but there are people, even there, who would leak for something as good as that. Or use it for political advantage." She paused for a few seconds. "And one of the names in there was mine. Hooke was blackmailing me, too."

Joy and I looked at each other, stunned. "Do you want to tell us why?" I finally asked.

She took a long breath and a longer pause. We waited impatiently.

"Hooke was accusing me of bribing a stableboy for inside information on a horse. It's not true, of course, but just the rumor made public would get me shunned by everybody in racing, and possibly even banned from the track. And racing is one of the few diversions I still have. It seemed easier to pay him the small sums he was demanding. That is rather the art of the blackmailer, isn't it, to only ask for as much as the victim will pay without breaking?"

The smart blackmailer at least, I thought. Who knew how much Accardo would press Ginnie if he got hold of the book.

"That settles it," I said. "I have to keep chasing the book."

"Yeah, I'm on board too," said Joy.

I was relieved. "I might even be able to decode it," I mused out loud.

"How?" asked Ginnie. "John spent hours on it, tried everything he knew, and got nowhere. I think he was getting close to throwing it on the fire."

I paused. "It's another long story, and one I'm not even supposed to tell, but here goes."

"Wait," said Ginnie, and poured more tea for all of us. A part of my brain wanted to know where the rich bought teapots that kept the tea warm for so long.

"I was a junior in college when Pearl Harbor happened. Not long after, the War Department came around advertising for girls who understood German or Japanese, liked crossword puzzles, and were single. Check, check, and check. German literature was my major. That was all they told us, and it sounded intriguing. So I volunteered. After interviews and aptitude tests and a stack of official paperwork, they told the few of us who passed what we had signed up for. We were going to be breaking Japan's and Germany's military codes. Strictly speaking, we were not supposed to talk about it for ten years, even though the war's over, so keep this to yourselves, okay?"

Joy and Ginnie both stared at me, astonished.

"Anyway, I jumped at the chance, and I have to tell you, it was the best two years of my life. We were doing something really important, but it was also a whole lot of fun for minds like ours. And there was an incredible camaraderie between the girls." Here I paused and looked at Joy. "You know what that was like, right?

She nodded.

I continued. "They shipped us all out to D.C. and put us at desks practically elbow to elbow. We worked in tight teams of six, cross-checking each other's work, sharing partial decodes back and forth, and there were friendly rivalries everywhere, within teams, between teams. Most of the work was Japanese, so the few of us working in German were even tighter. And when we weren't working, we were doing other puzzles. Competitive crossword solving. A lot of chess. Anything that looked like a puzzle, we were on it."

I looked at Joy again. "I have a small confession. I didn't learn lock picking sitting around the bookstore. A bunch of us decided a lock was basically a puzzle you could feel but not see, and set about teaching ourselves. We were pretty competitive about that, too. I never thought I'd use it for real, though. But the best part… the best part was being surrounded by girls like ourselves. None of us had ever had that before, and I doubt I'll ever have it again. We were not even supposed to contact each other after the war, for so-called security reasons." I was feeling wistful at the end there.

"I suppose they shut you down at the end of the war," said Joy. "Just like they did to us."

"Actually, no," I replied. "I had to leave at the end of '44. My father died suddenly. Heart attack. He was in the hospital for three days, but there was never any chance he'd wake up. So I had to leave the army and take over the bookstore. I never got to tell him what I'd been working on. And I never got to finish my degree."

"I'm sorry," said Ginnie. "About all of that."

Either she genuinely meant it, or they taught sincerity in good schools, too. "Thanks. But we don't always get to choose, do we? Anyway, the bottom line is, if we ever get our hands on the book, there is a very good chance I can crack it."

"Why would we want to?" asked Joy.

"There might be other people in there besides Ginnie who don't deserve to be blackmailed. We could let them know they were off the hook and can stop worrying. And we would probably need the coded details to identify them."

"That must have been what John was thinking, too," mused Ginnie.

"Now what?" I asked. "We're no closer to finding the book. We know Dalton didn't have it on him when Grayson snatched him, or Grayson wouldn't be coming to us. So Dalton must have stashed it somewhere. Not his office or his home, or at least anywhere we looked. But in hindsight, that seems too obvious, anyway. Maybe something that would keep it in circulation, never in one spot long enough for somebody else to find, like Joy's thought of mailing it back to himself. But I have no idea what."

I would have to sleep on that.

Chapter Thirteen

It was Tuesday evening and I was at Jack's bar again, drinking with a clutch of cab drivers. Besides us, the place was empty. I wondered whether the bar survived entirely on the drinking capacity of cabbies. I was sitting in what was now apparently my designated spot, squeezed between Joy and Madge. This was an experience I'd missed since leaving the army, a regular place, a regular spot, a regular group of people, and no expectations on me beyond showing up. I could get used to this.

Joy explained most of the men only came in for one drink before going home to wives and families. The ones who remained after seven were single, and mostly all they had to go home to was one room in a boarding house. I knew the feeling. It was well after seven now and I was just starting on my third shot. Some of the drivers waved to somebody over my shoulder, and I turned half-around to see Mikey coming in. He caught sight of me and blushed adorably.

He came over, put his hands on the back of my chair, lent down and whispered in my ear, "Dancing Thursday?" I touched his right hand with my left, looked up at him and nodded. So there it was. As casual as that, a second date. I made a mental note to wear my dancing skirt on Thursday. That would throw off my rotation, but it was more than worth it. Mikey took his beer around to the far side of the table and struck up a conversation, occasionally looking over at me with a shy smile.

After a while, I drifted off into thoughts of my own, losing track of the conversations going on around and across from me. We still had no leads on the book. And something was still bothering me about Dalton. Part of my brain, I was sure, knew what it was. I just wished it would let the rest of my brain know soon. Then it struck me. Something was off about what Joy had said. I came back to the conversations and waited for a break in Joy's chatter.

"Joy, I have to ask you something," I said. "When you drove Dalton around, where did he sit?"

"Always up front," said Joy. "Just like you do."

"Always?" I asked.

"Absolutely. I remember how weird it felt at first. Nobody had ever done it before. I had to ask Madge if it was even allowed. Took a week or more to get used to it."

"But you said the last time he saw Ginnie, he jumped in the back and slammed the door?"

"At least, that's the way Toby told it to me, yeah. Why, does it mean something?"

"I don't know yet," I replied. "I have to talk to Ginnie first. Is there a phone?"

Joy pointed me to the back, and I made my way between tables. There was a small, wooden half-booth which provided some approximation of privacy if you leaned in far enough and put your face close to the wall. I asked the operator to connect me, and she told me how much money to insert.

The line rang once, twice, then a lot more times before the operator came back on. "Miss, nobody is answering. I'm going to have to ask you to release the line."

I thanked her and hung up. My coins cascaded down into the cup and I put them back in my purse. Back at the table, Joy looked up at me expectantly.

I shook my head. "Nobody picked up. I guess she's out somewhere. I'll try again in the morning."

"You're not going to tell me?" she asked. She didn't look happy that I was keeping a secret.

I shook my head. "It's a half-thought and it might be completely wrong. I don't want to say anything until I'm sure." I finished my drink, said my goodbyes, and headed home. I didn't expect to sleep well, and I was right.

On Wednesday morning I waited impatiently at the store for the clock to tick around to nine. I figured if it wasn't too early for Ginnie to drink, it wasn't too early to call. Simmons picked up on the third ring, said, "Yes, Miss Stone," not entirely enthusiastically, and went in search of Ginnie.

After a few moments, I heard another phone pick up - I realized the house must have had more than one extension - and Ginnie's voice came on. "Is it okay if I ask you a few more questions about Dalton?" I asked.

"Of course," she replied.

"When he took a taxi to see you, did you notice where he sat?"

"That's an odd question," said Ginnie. "And the answer is a bit odd, too. He always sat up front next to the driver. Why?"

"I'm not there yet. A couple more questions. Do you know if he always used the same cab company?"

"Yes, Red Star. Their number is right here next to the phone. Is that important?"

"Yes. It's Joy's company. One last thing. The last time he visited you, did you see him leave?"

"I watched him from the window. You're going to ask me where he sat, and the answer is in the back. I was too mad to think anything of it at the time, but now you bring it up, it seems strange. Does it mean something?"

"It matches what I got from Joy. I have a theory. I think the last time Dalton saw you, he was already worried somebody was trying to take the book off of him. And I think he hid the book in the cab so it wouldn't be on him if it happened."

"Hid it? Where?" asked Ginnie.

"Down the back of the seat cushions, would be my guess. It would squeeze in there easily enough. Nobody would find it if they weren't looking for it, not even somebody cleaning the interior, and he could retrieve it in short order when he wanted."

"That's brilliant!" said Ginnie. "Constantly in circulation, just like you said."

To be frank, I was feeling pretty pleased with myself. "Now we just need to know which cab. I don't suppose you caught the cab's number or license plate?" I asked.

Ginnie laughed.

I took that as a No. Apparently, I was the only one who did that. "Okay," I sighed. "I guess we're going to have to search all of them."

My next call had to be to Madge. I didn't even know how many cabs Red Star had, let alone how we could possibly search them all. She told me to come over to the garage; she couldn't keep the dispatch phone tied up. The walk over did nothing to help my impatience, and closing the shop in the middle of the morning yet again wasn't helping to pay the bills - another hour, another two percent of my weekly take - so I was pretty keyed up by the time I got to the garage.

I'd never been inside the Red Star garage before. It was in the basement of an office building, accessed from the street by a steep ramp only wide enough for one car in or out, with a narrow, raised sidewalk along the side and no guardrail. I guessed it might once have been valet parking for the building itself. It was essentially a large, open, echoey concrete space with pillars widely-spaced. Fluorescent lights ran down the middle of the ceiling all the way from front to back with more around the walls.

The floor was spotted with pools of oil and water; where the two mixed, the surface sheened with hues of purple and turquoise. I tried my best not to step in any of them. The place smelled of gasoline and exhaust fumes. It was not somewhere I would want to work in all day. Just a few moments in there, and already I felt a headache coming on. I couldn't imagine how Madge could stand it.

Madge waved me over to the wood and glass booth she worked in. It gave an open view of the whole garage while providing a little insulation from the noise, but not the smell. She opened a window and I leaned in.

"I need help--" I started, when I was interrupted by the ringing of Madge's phone. I got a swift lesson in how she operated. She listened, punctuating the conversation with an occasional "uh huh" or "got it", and scribbled down the request from the customer. Then she hung up and promptly dialed out.

"There's cab ranks with phones all over the city," she explained while the phone rang, "And usually a couple of drivers hang around them when they're not cruising for fares." Somebody must have picked up because she launched into a rapid-fire description of the request, said "okay" to whatever she heard in return and hung up. I tried to get my request out before the phone rang again.

"I need to check the backs of all the cabs," I said as quickly as I could. "I think something important to Joy and me is hidden in one of them, pushed down the back of the seat."

The phone rang again, and Madge efficiently dispatched another request before turning back to me. "That sounds okay to me, but it's going to take time. I can't just call all the drivers and tell them to stop what they're doing, so you're going to have to wait for the cars to come back in at the end of a shift."

"And when is that?"

"Around six for the daytime shift. Sometimes a little earlier, often a little later," said Madge.

"That's not what I was hoping for," I said morosely. "But I'll just have to work with it." At least it meant I had no excuse not to open the store for the rest of the day.

"Maybe you should come back around five-thirty? That's the earliest the daytime guys start coming in and the evening shift starts to head out." The phone rang yet again, and Madge turned to take it.

I was taking all this in when I heard a welcome voice. It was Mikey. "I overheard some of that. Is it something I can help with?"

He seemed genuinely enthusiastic.

"Absolutely!" I said, beaming. "How many cabs are we talking about here?"

"Eighteen De Sotos, seven Fords, twenty-five total," he said promptly. "If we work the five-thirty to six-thirty shift change like Madge said, we can probably get most of them tonight and the rest tomorrow."

"Wow, you make it sound so easy," I remarked.

"I try. What do you need?"

"I think Dalton hid a notebook down the back of a seat, to keep it out of sight. Is it easy to pull out the cushions to look?"

"The De Sotos should be straightforward enough, they'll come right out. But for the Fords we'll need to take a couple of bolts out and lift up the seat."

"Why's that?" I asked, perplexed.

"The gap behind the seat opens to a space under the cushions for the springs," he explained. "If somebody pushed something between the cushion and the seat back, it would probably fall down there. Customers lose stuff there more often than you'd believe. Don't worry, it's not complicated, but it takes time and a socket wrench."

And probably more strength than I had, I thought. "Mikey, that would be great," I said. "If you can get off at five, let me buy you a drink at Jack's, and we can walk back over here for five-thirty."

He smiled and nodded his agreement. I was mildly surprised he agreed so readily to letting me buy a drink, but I guess the war - and well-paying jobs for women - had loosened a lot of older attitudes. I still didn't know what I was going to do if I did find the book.

I spent the rest of the day at the store, dividing my time between trying to make enough money to pay my rent and watching the clock crawl around towards five. My mind kept turning back to Accardo's thousand dollars, how much financial trouble it would erase for me, and how little I wanted to accept it.

Finally, at around fifteen minutes to five, I gave up, closed up the shop, and walked over to the bar, my umbrella shielding me from the inevitable afternoon rain. I was happy to see I had arrived before Mikey and accepted my usual rye from Jack. None of the other drivers were there yet, either, and I was happy at the thought Mikey and I might get some privacy. I was just lighting up my Kool when he came through the door. Jack reached for a mug and I told him to put it on my tab. He raised his eyebrows and looked over at Mikey, who just nodded. For the first time in my life, I had bought a man a drink. It felt good.

We sat up at a hightop. I always felt clumsy clambering up, but I liked being up high once I got there. We talked about going back to the same club on Thursday and whether the same band would be there. We talked about where to get dinner. We talked about what music we liked. We talked about nothing at all. With the time ticking around to five twenty, it was time to leave for the garage. I decided the clock in Jack's bar ran a lot faster than the one in my store.

We walked back over to the garage and I even allowed myself to feel creeping optimism that we were finally on the right track. It was a lot easier to be optimistic in Mikey's company. We got there at five thirty sharp. Madge was packing up for the day and she told us we hadn't missed any returns yet.

We told her we'd join her and the others at Jack's when we were done. A few minutes later, the first couple of cars, both De Sotos, came in and parked up, ready for the next shift. We took one each. It was easy enough to check the gap down the back of the seat, but we both came up empty. The third one in was a Ford, and Mikey directed it to the back of the garage.

"We'll deal with the Fords when the shift change is over. They'll take about ten or fifteen minutes each," he said.

"Won't the drivers need them?" I asked.

"No. We always have more cars than drivers in the evenings. And by midnight, fewer than half the cars might be out."

The cars came in pretty steadily, and so did the evening shift drivers, and we got into a good routine. Mikey directed traffic and I quickly searched each one after it came in. I kept careful track of the arrivals so Mikey didn't let one out before I'd checked it. The Fords were collecting at the back. By six thirty, we'd checked all the De Sotos, and all but three of them were back out on the road. It didn't look like any more drivers were going to check in. We had the garage to ourselves.

"Okay," said Mikey. "Let's try the Fords."

All seven Fords were lined up at the back. Mikey opened up a large, metal cupboard and brought out a long ratchet and a couple of sockets. I watched as he worked on the first car. It took all his weight to get the bolt started, but afterward, it came pretty easily. He came around the other side and did the same.

Taking one end of the bench seat each, we lifted it forward and up. It was heavy, but between us, we managed alright. Mikey had been right: underneath the seat was a hollow, and all sorts of junk had accumulated there. Small change, combs, a billfold too late to return, some toy metal soldiers, a filthy handkerchief, but no black leather notebook.

"One down, six to go," said Mikey, undaunted. We tilted the seat back into place and Mikey tightened up the bolts. Before we could open the doors on the next one, we heard footsteps echoing through the garage. This was not a place anybody could sneak into. A large man in an ill-fitting dark suit walked towards us. Mikey went out to meet him. As they got close, I realized just how big the man was, inches taller than Mikey, and built like a beer truck.

"Sir, you can't be in here," Mikey said politely but firmly.

"It's okay," said the man. "I'm a friend of Miss Stone."

His voice was deep and gravelly and not friendly at all. Mikey turned to look at me and I shook my head emphatically. He turned back to the man, but before he could say anything, the thug planted his fist into his midriff. It was the punch of a man who meant to do harm and knew how to do it. Mikey doubled over, coughed, and tried to straighten up. He brought up his right arm, the ratchet still in it, but before he could swing it, the man caught his wrist in his massive left hand and with his right, punched Mikey on the ear. Mikey's legs buckled and he stumbled. Only the man's grip on his right wrist kept him upright.

He got his legs under himself and looked up at the man, obviously dazed. The man took his time, picked his spot, landed a punch on Mikey's temple. The ratchet fell from Mikey's hand. It hit the ground, bounced, and landed again. The ringing reverberated up and down the garage. Mikey was a rag doll now. The man let go of him and he folded to the ground in a pile. The man poked him with his boot and drew his leg back to kick him hard in the side. Mikey lifted into the air an inch or two and fell back. He didn't make a sound and he didn't move. I was shocked, terrified, and trembling. My limbs would not obey my brain.

Suddenly, I unfroze. I ran the half dozen steps towards Mikey. The man stepped over Mikey's inert body, putting himself between Mikey and myself. He reached out a hand and planted it on my shoulder. I stopped so hard my feet almost went from under me. Standing there under the harsh, fluorescent lights, I got a good look at his face. It could certainly be described as a boxer's face. Scars from old cuts fringed his eyes, and there was more scar tissue along his cheekbones. His nose had been broken at least twice, and his jaw looked like it didn't quite sit right.

And he had a scar from the corner of his right eye down his cheek and past his mouth. "Moretti," I managed to get out.

"Nice to meet you, Miss Stone," he replied. He wasn't even breathing heavily from his exertion. "Mr. Accardo wanted me to remind you he's waiting for his book."

I stared up at him for several seconds deciding how much of a lie I could get away with. I was guessing he didn't want to hit me unless he had to or he would have done so by now.

Or maybe he was just afraid of hitting me too hard and accidentally breaking me.

"I don't have it," I said. I could hear my voice trembling. "It's inside a panel in one of those cars, and you just laid out the only man who knows how to open them up."

Moretti looked hard at me, taking this in. He glanced over his shoulder at Mikey's body, still slumped and unmoving, maybe wondering if he could slap him awake. I didn't think it was a good idea, but I was pretty sure my opinion on the matter didn't count for much. After a couple of seconds, he looked back at me.

"He should be able to work again in a couple of days. I'll give you three to come up with the book. Otherwise, we have to do this over again. And maybe next time, I'll give you a bit of a slap, too." To punctuate his point he gave a firm shove on my shoulder, and I went down hard on my backside.

He turned and walked away, making a show of stepping over Mikey's body again. As he hit the ramp out of the garage, I rolled over on my knees and scooted over to Mikey. My hands were grazed and my skirt was dirty and my stockings were wrecked and I didn't care. I put my head down low to his body. His breath was slow and shallow. I didn't like the sound of it at all. I picked myself up and ran again, now to the dispatch booth. Inside, I grabbed the phone, dialed the operator and asked for a hospital with an emergency room. I went back to Mikey to wait for the ambulance. As I knelt there, I desperately wanted to hold him, but the rational part of my brain told me not to move him. Instead, I just took his hand in mine and whispered, "Help's coming."

I hoped he could hear me.

Chapter Fourteen

I rode in the ambulance with Mikey, the siren wailing frantically above my head. His breathing was still shallow and the nurse watched him anxiously, occasionally glancing out the front window to see how close we were. Her obvious anxiety was not helping my own state of mind. Pulling up at the hospital, the nurse, driver, and two orderlies lifted him onto a gurney and wheeled him into the back, banging carelessly through a pair of double doors which swung back and forth twice before settling closed, leaving me sitting alone and fidgeting in the waiting room.

I stayed there, watching doctors and nurses and orderlies come and go for a couple of hours. The room was cold and unadorned, the chairs stiff and unyielding. It felt like the room was designed to discourage waiting. Other patients came in from time to time, and their friends and families waited a while. Sometimes, we would smile grimly at each other and nod to acknowledge our common helplessness. Doctors came out and whispered to them, and then they left.

Eventually around ten o'clock, a doctor came out and talked to me. Mikey was still unconscious, he said, but breathing better. He had two broken ribs and a ruptured eardrum. He almost certainly had a concussion, but they wouldn't know how bad until he was awake and responsive. His torso was heavily bruised, but as far as they could tell, there were no internal injuries or bleeding. And none of his facial bones seemed broken. They were going to keep him in for observation, at least until he was conscious. Apparently, this was relatively good news.

I went back to waiting. I must have fluttered in and out of a light doze, because more time passed than I could account for; but the chair was too uncomfortable to sleep for long. The hands of the clock ground past midnight.

Sometime around two in the morning, a nurse shook me awake. At first, I was disoriented, but after a moment, I remembered where I was and why.

"Mr. Eastman is conscious right now, but probably not for long," she said. "Normally, the ward is closed for visitors at this hour, but if you're quiet and don't wake anybody else, you can have a couple of minutes."

The nurse showed me to a general ward with two dozen beds. I stepped out of my shoes, and in my stockinged feet, walked silently to his bed. She had warned me his face looked bad but it looked worse than it really was. She was right. There was a bruise the size of an apple on his temple where Moretti had punched him, and the blue and purple spread up beyond his hairline and down to his cheekbone.

She had also told me he couldn't focus too well just yet and he was not entirely coherent, so if he said anything strange, to just ignore it. And she had warned me by tomorrow, he might not remember anything about my visit. As I stood next to him, he made an exaggerated attempt to raise his head and hold it steady, squinting at me. He laid it back down on the pillow, puffing painfully.

"Dot?" he whispered.

I came up alongside him and kissed him very gently on the side of his face that was not an ugly turquoise color.

"That had better be Dot," he said.

He was at least a bit coherent, I concluded. "How are you feeling?" I asked.

"Like I stepped in front of a streetcar," he muttered. "Actually, a streetcar would probably have been kinder." I laughed and winced in equal measure.

"Does this mean you aren't taking me dancing tonight?" I asked. He laughed lightly, then spasmed in pain, and with a heavy breath out, he lay back.

"Sorry," I whispered. I took his hand and held it for a while, just sitting quietly with him and listening to his breathing grow steady. His eyes were closed and he might have been asleep again. I hoped it was real sleep rather than the terrifying unconsciousness I had seen in the garage.

After a couple of minutes, the nurse came by and told me she was sorry but it was time for me to leave. She walked me out of the ward and and started to explain care procedures to me. Once he was discharged, I should ice his bruises as much as possible and not allow him to exert himself in ways which would require heavy breathing, although the pain would probably quickly dissuade him from it, anyway. And I should keep an eye on the concussion. No driving or operating machinery for at least a week, even though he might think he was better. And symptoms like dizziness and nausea might come and go. He could feel fine one day and worse the day after. Apparently, she had decided we were a couple. I wasn't sure how I felt about that.

"Can't I stay in case he wakes up again?" I asked. I had no idea what I could do, but I wanted to be there.

"Sorry, but no," said the nurse. "You won't be allowed back in the ward until visiting hours tomorrow. The best thing you can do for him right now is go home, get some sleep, and save your energy so you can take care of him."

I figured I could do one of those things. There was a cab rank outside the hospital, and by chance, a Red Star cab was waiting. I walked over to the driver and he put down his newspaper. I introduced myself as Joy's friend and asked how much it would cost to get home. To my surprise, he knew who I was; apparently, word had gotten around even the midnight shift drivers that Mikey had a girlfriend. He asked what I was doing at the hospital and I told him about Mikey. He looked shocked and told me no charge for the ride. I didn't protest; I almost certainly didn't have enough money to get home.

I undressed and lay in bed, staring at the ceiling, my thoughts an anxious whirl of fear, anger and anxiety, replaying Moretti's brutal attack and his threats, the ride to the hospital, and how Mikey had looked in the hospital bed. Despite my physical exhaustion, my thoughts would not settle.

I must have drifted off eventually because my alarm clock jolted me awake. All my worries of the previous night immediately came flooding back. I got to the garage early, well before eight. Madge's dispatch booth was empty, so I borrowed her seat while I waited. I felt drained both physically and mentally, but knew it was nothing compared to what Mikey must be feeling.

Madge walked in at about a quarter of eight. She saw me and waved. I came out of the booth and met her at the bottom of the ramp. I told her all about Mikey, stopping repeatedly for her questions. Her face mixed anger and concern. While I was telling the story, a couple of drivers showed up and I stopped and restarted for them. More drivers arrived, and they passed the word around among themselves. Faces registered shock, disbelief, anger, anxiety. Some were talking heatedly about what they would do if they caught the man who did it. Having seen Moretti at work, I reflected it would probably take all of them.

Madge pulled me aside. "Do you know what he wanted?" she asked.

"It was because of the thing Joy and I were looking for. His mobster boss wants it, too. If Mikey hadn't volunteered to help, he wouldn't even have been here last night."

"I hope you're not going to do something stupid like blame yourself," said Madge. "There's only one person responsible for this."

"My brain knows it," I said. "It's the rest of me that needs persuading."

"The question is, what are you going to do now?"

"I don't really know. But first, we get the book. I'll figure out later what to do with it. I'm going to need one of the guys to help, though."

Madge waved over one of the drivers, introduced him as Geoff, and we made our way to the back of the garage where the Fords were still parked. Half a dozen drivers followed us to see what was going on. The ratchet was still lying on the ground where Mikey had dropped it. I picked it up and gave it to Geoff.

"Mikey undid two screws--" I started to say.

"You mean bolts," said Geoff.

"What's the difference?" I asked.

Geoff looked at me for a few seconds before deciding how patronizing to be. "Screws are pointy. Bolts are blunt."

I wished I hadn't asked. "Two bolts," I continued. "This one here, and the same on the other side." I explained the rest. Like Mikey, Geoff had to put all his weight on the ratchet to get the bolt started. He repeated the exercise for the second one. We lifted the seat and found a similar assortment of junk and loose change to the one Mikey and I had opened. We put the seat back and Geoff tightened up the bolts.

We got lucky on the next one. There was the notebook, just as Joy had first described it to me. It was greasy and dirty with hair and dust and gum stuck to it, but unmistakably what we were looking for. I pulled a handkerchief from my purse and used it to pick up the book. I flicked through. Sure enough, there was a page for Grayson. And another for Townsend. And pages for several people who happened to share a last name with some prominent local politicians and businessmen. There were even a couple of well-known Hollywood figures, or possibly by great coincidence, their namesakes. Every page in code, just as Ginnie had described it.

"That little thing's what this is all about?" asked Geoff, incredulously.

"Yes," I answered coolly. "I know it doesn't look like much, but some very dangerous people are willing to do some very violent things to get it."

I heard a cheerful voice from behind me.

"Hey, you found our Maltese Falcon!"

It was Joy. "If that means the notebook, then yes," I replied.

She clapped me on the arm and looked me in the eyes. "How are you doing?" she asked.

"Me? I'm freaking out about Accardo, I'm mad as heck at Moretti, and I'm concerned about Mikey. And I'm worrying how you're handling the news about Dalton. How do I look?"

"Pretty good, considering. Now what?"

"I don't know," I said. "I suppose I could give Grayson his page, which is what he said he wanted, although I'm not sure I believe him now. I could cut out and destroy Ginnie's page. And I could give the rest of the book to Accardo," I said.

"And then it would be over."

"For us, it would be. Not for the rest of the people listed in the book. And not for Mikey. I feel like there has to be a settling of accounts for that. But I have no idea how. I don't see where we have any leverage."

"So, what's next?" she asked.

"I need some time to figure it out. I'm hoping the lie I told Moretti will buy us a couple of days. In the meantime, I need to put this--" I held up the book. "--somewhere safe." I carefully wrapped the filthy book in my handkerchief and dropped it into my purse.

"You have somewhere in mind?" she asked.

"I have somewhere nobody will ever think to look. Can you drive me over to Dalton's office?"

Joy nodded. A pedantic part of my brain annotated, Dalton's former office, and I told it to shut up.

Fifteen minutes later, we were parked in front, and I still hadn't seen signs of a tail. I wanted to believe that meant both Accardo and Grayson had kept their words, however unlikely it seemed. Inside, Ángel was sitting on a small, three-legged stool and reading the newspaper. He smiled to see us, and we exchanged hellos.

"Three?" he asked. The two of us said 'Yes' in concert.

The door to Dalton's office was locked again. There was also a notice on it with POLICE in big bold letters at the top. Underneath in smaller letters, it explained the office was a crime scene and nobody could go inside without authorization. Neither the lock nor the notice applied to us, it turned out.

Inside, a few things had changed. There was a dark black stain on the rug where the body had been lying. I tried not to think about the previous scene. The door to the inner office was unlocked, and I put my bobby pins back in my hair, tucking away a loose strand or two. In the back room, more had happened. It looked like somebody had searched the place, presumably the police. The drawers on the desk had been left open as well as the bottom drawer of the leftmost filing cabinet, the only one with files in it.

A sweep of dust was missing from the corner of the desk, like somebody had sat there. Out of curiosity, I picked up the phone. The line was dead. I assumed Dalton hadn't paid his bill.

"Now what?" asked Joy. I could tell she didn't want to be in here any more than I did. I dropped the book into the bottom desk drawer, the one with the stack of unpaid bills, and closed both drawers.

"That's it?" she said. "That's your great hiding place?"

"Sure," I replied. "Who's going to look in a place everybody has already searched?"

Joy stared at me for a few seconds. "Damn. That's brilliant," she finally said.

"Thank you."

"So we can go now?"

"Not just yet," I said. "There's something I want to check." I went over to the filing cabinet and closed the bottom drawer so I could open the top one without it falling on me. Joy sat down in Dalton's chair and started swiveling back and forth while tapping one finger on the desktop. It was annoying as heck, but I didn't want to say anything.

I flicked through the manilla folders in the top drawer, and like Joy had said the first time we'd been there, there was no obvious order to them. Each one was labeled with a name, but they certainly were not alphabetical. I looked inside a few and saw they all had at least one piece of paper: an engagement agreement, signed and dated by Dalton and the client. It was obvious now. The labels on the folders were the clients' names, and they were arranged chronologically, the most recent in the top drawer at the front.

The Hooke case had been about three months back, which took me back just four folders. Dalton really had not been doing a lot of business lately. But something was missing. Right where the Hooke case should be, there was a gap of almost three weeks. There was an adultery case more than a week before Hooke's death, then nothing until an insurance fraud case, obviously nothing to do with Hooke. Had somebody been here before us and taken the Hooke folder? I stared into the distance. I didn't see what else it could be.

"Satisfied?" asked Joy, needlessly impatiently, I thought.

"Kind of. I have something to think about, but we can get out of here now."

We walked back down to the lobby where Ángel was once again immersed in his paper. Joy interrupted him to give him two dollars, which he accepted gracefully and added to the brown bag under his stool.

"Thank you again," she said.

"For what?" said Ángel, grinning. "You weren't even here."

Joy dropped me back at my store with a promise to pick me up at four so we could go visit Mikey, and an agreement to go for a drink afterwards.

There wasn't much to do for the rest of the day. I called Ginnie, but Simmons said she was out. I asked him to tell her we had found the book, and she would know what that meant.

I hoped some customers would come in and break up the waiting.

Chapter Fifteen

Our trip to the hospital was fruitless. The nurse told us Mikey had briefly woken up at around ten that morning. He had been lucid and they had given him something for the pain. He had eaten some broth and had promptly thrown it up. She assured us this was all completely normal with severe concussions. He was sleeping again, and she wouldn't allow us to disturb him. They had decided to keep him in for another night.

We went back to the bar and waited for the other drivers to drift in. We shared the update, such as it was. The mood was subdued, not surprisingly. I had one more shot of rye than was probably good for me, hoping I could walk it off on the way home. I picked at dinner, went to bed, and slept fitfully. I couldn't shake the feeling this was at least partly my fault - and worse, maybe some of the drivers thought so, too.

The next morning at the store was slow. I was about to wish it had stayed that way. The phone rang, and since no customers were in the store, I went into the office and answered it. It was Madge. She didn't say much.

"Stay where you are. Joy is coming to pick you up."

I started to ask what it was all about but she hung up. Right. Can't keep the dispatch phone tied up. I turned the sign on the door to Closed - I flinched at the thought of more lost sales - and put my coat on. I went out to the curb to wait, locking the door behind me. Joy pulled up just a few minutes later. I walked around the car and slid into the front seat.

"Say 'hi'," she said, jerking her thumb to the back seat. I twisted around and was surprised to see Ángel sitting there. He raised a hand in greeting.

"What the heck is going on?" I asked nobody in particular.

"Somebody broke into Mr. Dalton's office. You have to come see," said Ángel. I immediately assumed the worst. We sat in silence the rest of the way. At Dalton's office, Ángel took us up to the third floor.

"I'll hold the elevator for you," he said.

"What if somebody needs it?" the rules-obsessed part of my brain insisted that I ask.

Ángel shrugged. "They can walk. Or they can wait."

Standing in front of Dalton's office door, it was clear that whoever had broken in didn't care who knew. The lock hadn't been picked, it had just been kicked open. There was a footprint-sized dent in the wood of the door and the frame was splintered. Inside, the door to the inner office stood open.

I went straight to the drawer where I'd stashed the notebook. Of course it was gone. I'd had my hands on it for less than one day. "Damn it," I said. I slumped heavily into the chair behind the desk.

I scowled. "What are we going to do now?"

"I have no idea," Joy said. "But I know you'll think of something."

I wished I had her confidence.

"Right now, though, we have to get out of here," she added. She was right.

We returned to the elevator and Ángel took us back down. Nobody was waiting.

"Did you see who might have done this?" I asked.

"Oh, for certain," he said. "An anglo, about my height, black hair, very slick, and an old suit." I looked at Joy, and it was obvious we were both suspecting the same thing: although the description was broad, we were both thinking of the man who had accosted us at Dalton's apartment. If only we knew who he worked for, that would be something.

"He went upstairs, I heard a big crash, a couple of minutes later he came back down," said Ángel. "Didn't even look at me. Didn't care that I saw him. I went up to check, thinking it might be to do with Dalton, and for sure, it was. Right away, I thought you ladies needed to know about this. I didn't know what else to do, so I took the streetcar over to the Red Star garage."

"Thanks, Ángel," Joy said.

"It's nothing," he replied in his trademark growl. "But if you ladies could leave now, I need to call the police."

Joy drove me back to the store. Neither of us spoke the whole way. As she pulled up in front, I sighed heavily.

"What do you think?" she asked.

"Somebody must have followed us there and figured out what I did. Apparently, we're not as good at spotting a tail as we thought."

"So what's the plan now?" said Joy.

"I don't know," I said despondently. "This week cannot get any worse." The week was about to prove me spectacularly wrong.

I told Joy I'd meet her at the bar after work and maybe I would have an idea by then. I climbed out and watched her drive away, deep in my own thoughts. She didn't get far before two men flagged her down at the corner of the next block. She stopped and waited while they squeezed into the back, then pulled out again. She stopped at the end of the block, made a right, and disappeared from my sight.

And then my brain poked me: one of the men had been about the height and build of Moretti. My stomach turned to stone.

I spent the next two hours alternately convincing and unconvincing myself that it was just a coincidence, there were lots of big men in Los Angeles. Half of them were playing heavies in mob pictures. Surely there was no reason for Moretti to get into Dot's cab, he'd already frightened me enough. I thought about calling the police and dismissed the idea almost immediately. What was I going to say? "My taxi driver friend picked up a fare and I think he might be a mobster. No, I don't know why or where they might have gone." All I could do was sit and wait. Wait until Joy showed up at the bar later as agreed, her usual happy self. Or some messenger from Accardo showed up to explain why he'd grabbed Joy.

I decided to leave the Closed sign up. I couldn't deal with customers in the state I was in, however badly I needed the money. I turned out the lights in the store and sat in my office, staring at my accounts ledger and trying to find some mathematical magic that would make it add up to making my rent and buying food, too. Right now, Accardo's thousand dollars seemed like the only way, but I liked the idea even less now than the first time I heard it. Hours and minutes and seconds dragged by.

Around four-thirty, I heard a knocking at the door. What kind of idiot couldn't take a hint from a dark storefront and a Closed sign, I thought with annoyance. I ignored it. It came again, and I ignored it again. It came a third time, and I realized the light from my office must be spilling out into the store.

Sighing dramatically for the benefit of nobody but myself, I pushed back from the desk and walked out of my office. Standing at the door was Grayson. I thought about turning around and going back into my office, and then I thought about Dalton's office door. I didn't feel like having to get my door repaired a second time this month, and I didn't think he was going away. I opened the door to him and he pushed inside. Right behind him was the slick-haired man from Dalton's apartment. He was holding a gun. This was the second time he'd pointed a gun at me, and I didn't like it any better than the first time. I leaned right and peered behind him theatrically. He jerked around; luckily for him, Joy wasn't there. He glared at me.

"Miss Stone, you're going to come with us," Grayson said. "Please do so quietly so my friend Colt here doesn't have to hurt you."

I thought that Colt would probably enjoy that, possibly Grayson, too. They each took an arm and between them, pulled and pushed me through the door. The same black DeSoto I'd ridden in before was parked at the curb. I was disappointed. I'd expected Grayson to have something much classier for his own use. Maybe the hospitality business wasn't going so great. Everybody had money problems, it seemed.

He bundled me into the back and pulled out a gun of his own. He waved it around vaguely; he didn't seem nearly as sure what to do with it as Colt did. Colt put his away and slid behind the wheel. Before long, I had an idea where we were heading: Grayson's restaurant up in the hills. Colt was a much better driver than the ferret-faced man who had driven me before, but that didn't make the drive any more comfortable. I kept quiet for the whole trip. Grayson didn't seem in the mood for flirting.

Colt pulled the car around the side to the parking lot. Concealed by a thick hedge about six feet high, there was a metal door on the side of the building - service and delivery entrance, I guessed. I was right. The door led into a locker room and from there, into the kitchen. The two of them marched me through. A couple of white-jacketed men briefly looked up from prepping vegetables, but didn't pay any more attention. I assumed they were paid not to. There didn't seem much mileage in my making a fuss; it would probably only get me hurt.

Two swing doors exited the kitchen. I guessed the one to the right led to the restaurant, the left to the casino, perhaps a holdover from its earlier incarnation as a speakeasy. We went left.

I had figured out where we were going just in time for it not to matter. Sure enough, inside the casino, Grayson left me in Colt's grip while he went over to one of the wall panels. I noticed now it didn't quite fit seamlessly. He pushed on the edge of the panel, and I was unsurprised to see it swing inwards, revealing a stub of a corridor and a second door that opened into another room. The room was large enough to hold maybe thirty people if they didn't mind getting intimately acquainted. I deduced it was a hiding place from the days when this had been a speakeasy, and it accounted for the missing floorspace that had been nagging at my brain.

If there was a police raid back in the day, I guessed the more privileged patrons would gather in here while the police conducted their business. Or at least pretended to. I assumed the cops back then were every bit as amenable to a payoff as they apparently were these days, and any raids would be just for the show of the thing. Who knows, I thought. Maybe for some of the patrons, the thrill of a close escape from a raid was part of the pleasure. The outer door closed behind us with a solid thud that brooked no misinterpretation.

The room was dimly lit by a single pendant light. In the middle of the room was a high-backed wooden chair, and standing next to it was a hard-faced woman in a tight-fitting black woolen dress. She was beyond thin and on her way to skeletal. She seemed to be assembled entirely from points and edges. Her skin was stretched taut over her cheekbones and the creases around her mouth and forehead suggested somebody who frowned more than smiled. The look of somebody used to disappointment. The harshness of her makeup did nothing to help. Her pose was stiff, tightly coiled, and even her patent leather heels looked uncomfortably tight at the toes. I couldn't decide if it was the alertness of predator or prey; of pounce or flee. Her hair was mostly blonde, of a shade not found in nature, with dark roots overdue for touching up. A poor man's idea of a tough girl, I thought uncharitably.

From the tips of the fingers of her right hand, swinging gently back and forth, she dangled a pair of handcuffs. It was all a little too theatrical for my liking. I blamed Hollywood mob pictures for setting a bad example.

Colt and Grayson stood me in front of her, turned me around, and held my arms behind my back. She fastened the handcuffs to one of my wrists, tighter than was really necessary, I felt. They turned me back around. For the first time since he had forced me into the car, Grayson opened his mouth.

"Nice, isn't?" he said, his sweeping arm taking in the room. "You can scream for help if you want, it's very thoroughly soundproofed."

"What's this about, Anthony? I thought we were partners," I replied. I deliberately mispronounced his name, and also resolved to have a word later with the part of my brain that thought this was a good time to tweak him. He pushed me down hard into the chair, which scooted back a couple of inches with the force of my impact. He fed the handcuffs around one of the curved rods that made up the back of the chair and attached them to my other wrist. The three of them stood side by side now, looking down at me.

"I thought so, too," he replied. "Until you involved yourself with Accardo."

I wanted to protest that it was hardly by choice, but this time I had the self-control to keep my thoughts to myself.

"Anyway," he continued. "I decided to help myself to the book before Accardo got his hands on it." He reached inside his suit coat and pulled out the notebook. He'd had somebody thoroughly clean it up before allowing it anywhere near his suit, I noted.

"You said you only wanted your own page," I protested.

"I lied," he replied. "That happens a lot. But it was endearingly sweet of you to have believed me. I always intended to take the whole thing off your hands once you found it for me."

I gave him my best glare, which apparently was still not very good. "Aren't you worried about Accardo?" I asked. "It seems like he could take it from you without too much trouble."

"Not at all. Several of Accardo's political friends are in here. It would be extremely damaging for his business interests if they were exposed and forced to resign. It might even force the city to take action against Accardo, at least for appearances' sake."

"That sounds like a good reason for him to have you bumped off, as they say in the movies," I said. "Moretti seems to be quite keen on that sort of thing."

"Indeed. The trick is to have copies made of the key pages and let Accardo know they are stashed safely with friends, in case anything should happen to me."

"It sounds like you've thought of everything," I said.

"Everything but one," he replied. "There is just the small problem that the book is in code. Fortunately, you're going to decode it for me."

"I don't think I am," I replied flatly.

He turned to Colt.

"Hit her once. Not too hard. Just to motivate her a little better," Grayson said. He waved Colt forward with a two-fingered gesture. This seemed like an odd moment to notice how beautifully manicured his nails were.

"What?" Colt said. "I ain't never hit a woman before!"

"First time for everything, Colt."

"But it don't seem right," he replied. His face was contorted with distaste.

"She hit you with a blackjack! You're still limping!"

"That was the other one," he said miserably.

"I don't care. Just get on with it," said Grayson, angry now.

Still looking deeply reluctant, Colt stepped up to me. He balled his right hand into a fist, pulled it back, and stopped there, his body and his mind frozen in opposition. After a couple of seconds, he un-balled his fist and lowered his hand. "Sorry boss," he said. "I just can't."

The woman let out a loud "Tsk", shouldered past him, raised her bony right hand, and slapped me hard across the left cheek with a loud smack that I heard from inside my head as much as outside. So hard it snapped my head all the way around to the right.

I gasped loudly. I'd never been hit in the face before, and I was astonished at how shocking it felt. I'd never imagined anything like it no matter how often I'd seen it in the movies. My whole cheek was burning. Inside my mouth was a bright, coppery taste. I'm probably bleeding, I thought. I straightened my head and looked up at her, my face a mixture of anger and fear. Before I could react any further, she backhanded me across the other cheek. Her knuckles hurt even more than her palm had. I felt a sting to my cheek and then a warm trickle. She's cut me with one of her rings, I thought. I wonder if I'll have a scar. Absurdly, I worried that the blood might stain my blouse. My right ear was ringing, and my head felt muzzy. Was this what a concussion felt like? My mind drifted to Mikey, still lying in his hotel bed.

"Thank you, Dolores," said Grayson, not betraying any surprise at what he had just witnessed. "Let's leave Miss Stone to consider her position for a while." They left the way they had come in, the outer door thudding shut.

I sat quietly for a few minutes. It wasn't just the pain that had shocked me. It was the cold use of violence as a first resort. I had measured Grayson as a vain, foppish, slightly foolish man, but obviously I had underestimated him. And overestimated myself. I wriggled my hands and wrists to keep them from going to sleep, felt the stinging of pins and needles as they woke up.

I simply couldn't see any way out of this. I could push back, depending on how much pain I was willing to tolerate, but eventually, I was going to have to decode the notebook for Grayson and hope that was an end to it as far as my involvement was concerned. Grayson and Accardo could fight it out after that. Unless one or other decided I knew too much and should disappear. I had no idea what would happen to Joy then, or Ginnie.

Some time passed, I had no way of knowing how much. I might even have drifted into some approximation of dazed sleep for a while. I jerked awake to the sound of the door thumping closed again. It was Grayson and Dolores. Apparently, Colt had been relegated to other chores.

"Dolores, would you give Miss Stone a little reminder?" said Grayson.

"With pleasure," she replied. Her voice matched her face: sharp, and shopworn.

"Wait--" I started to say, but she wasn't interested. She brought her hand back and slapped me on the left cheek again. I tried to jerk my head out of the way, but only succeeded in losing my balance. Grayson and Dolores watched indifferently as I tottered, tried to straighten up, and then fell sideways, landing heavily on my right shoulder. I groaned in pain. I looked up at Dolores and Grayson, helpless. After a moment, they stepped forward and manhandled me upright again. I tried and failed to swallow a quiet moan.

They turned and walked away. Apparently, they didn't care whether or not I was ready to cooperate. I was struggling to come to terms with the casual cruelty. My eyes stung with tears.

The door slammed shut behind them.

Chapter Sixteen

I sat as still as I could, waiting for my eyes to stop stinging and trying to consciously settle my breathing. Nobody was coming, I thought. Nobody even knew I was here.

I had to do something more than sit in despair.

I tried to ignore the bruised shoulder, the muzzy head, the ringing ear, and the ache every time I moved my jaw. I could still taste blood. I probed my teeth with my tongue, hoping Dolores hadn't broken one for me; I certainly couldn't afford a dentist this month.

Decoding the book for Grayson meant abandoning Joy to Accardo, so that was a non-starter. But I couldn't just wait around to see how many times Dolores wanted to slap me before she got bored.

The handcuffs were hugely frustrating. They were the easiest things in the world to pick, provided, of course, you had a lockpick in your hand. Which I didn't.

I didn't need a plan, I told myself. I just needed a first step.

If I could get free of the chair, it at least would be something. I gave a frustrated jerk on the handcuffs, hoping perhaps the rod I was chained to might miraculously break. It didn't, but I did get painful scrapes on both my wrists to add to my list of pains. I grabbed the rod behind my back and gave it an experimental push backwards - nothing - and then a twist. To my surprise, it moved a fraction. Grasping it with both hands, I started twisting it back and forth. The twisting was blistering up the fingers on both my hands, but it didn't matter; it moved a fraction more each time. Suddenly, it was rotating freely.

Now what, I asked myself. The rods curved backwards, I reasoned. Maybe if I could bend it far enough, it would pop out of its sockets. I pushed as hard as I could with both hands and felt it give a little, not much, and not nearly enough. Cuffed, I had so little leverage.

I hooked my feet around the legs of the chair and pushed again with all my weight and the strength of my legs. I felt it give more, and suddenly it sprang free. The rebound of the rod smacked me hard in the left kidney and I cried out loudly, then it clattered to the floor. The sudden release jolted through my shoulder, squeezing a couple of tears from the corners of my eyes. A good thing this room was soundproof, I thought.

I caught my breath again. As much as I wanted to curl up in a corner and cry, it would have to come later. I had no idea when Grayson and Dolores would be back for round three.

This was progress, I told myself, but not nearly there yet. Next step. Somehow, I had to get my hands in front of me. I knelt down and leaned forward, my knees crushed up to my chest as far as I could manage, my forehead on the floor. I could barely breathe. All I needed to do now was somehow pass my feet over the chain, but my arms were too short by an inch or more to get the chain over my heels. Idiot, I told myself, and kicked my shoes off.

Now I was close; I could almost squeeze my left heel through if I could compress the flesh just that bit more. I twisted my shoulders around to the left, strained as far as I could, and the chain jerked forward over my left heel. As it did so I felt something tear inside my right shoulder. I squealed in pain again, but my foot slipped through. The second foot followed easily.

My shoulder was burning fiercely. I ignored it. I plucked a bobby pin from my hair, popped the cuffs open, and slipped them into the pocket of my skirt. A fleeting moment of satisfaction. I put my shoes back on.

Keep moving while the adrenaline is still flowing, I told myself. This is all going to hurt a lot once it stops. What next? I looked around the room, but all I saw was featureless panels like the ones in the casino. No convenient, hidden door to the car park. The only way out seemed to be the door Grayson and Dolores had used. It would land me in the casino; would it be busy now? I had no real idea what time it was. The way I probably looked, if anybody was there, it would surely cause a commotion which would bring Grayson running. I needed a bigger head start if I were to get away.

I didn't have a choice. One more step and see what happened. I gathered my courage and approached the outer door. I put my ear against it and listened; nothing. I eased it open; still silence. I stepped into the empty casino, grateful a morsel of fortune was finally on my side, crossed the room and went through the swing door to the kitchen. There were more chefs working, the kitchen filled with steam and shouts and the dissonant clang of pans and knives, but they paid as little attention to me on the way out as they had on the way in. Not their business to care what the boss was up to. Maybe bruised and scraped women came through the kitchen all the time.

I slipped outside. Judging by the low light and the long shadows, it was around six o'clock. I crept to the corner of the hedge and peered around. There was the parking lot, and a dozen cars sat there. Apparently the diners arrived earlier than the gamblers. As I watched, a valet brought another car around from the front and parked it on the end of the row. I pulled back from the corner to avoid being seen. He took the keys out of the ignition, and to my surprise, shoved them above the sun visor. He jogged away.

I took stock of the cars sitting there, a mix of shiny, late model sedans belonging to the customers and a handful of older, beaten-up vehicles presumably belonging to the staff. I needed something easy to handle: my right shoulder was throbbing distractingly now and I didn't want to deal with anything with heavy steering. A 1940 Ford Deluxe Coupe caught my eye. I walked over, trying to look confident in case another valet showed up. I slipped inside, found the keys behind the visor, turned the ignition to on and pushed the starter button.

It turned over and caught first time. I breathed out; I hadn't even realized I had been holding my breath. I kicked off my shoes again. It was going to be easier to drive in my stockings than heels. I put the car into reverse and winced as pain shot through my right shoulder again. I backed out slowly and clumsily jammed the gearbox into first with a sickening crunch of clashing gears. I hadn't driven since I'd left the army two years ago, and now nervous energy, fear, and adrenaline were all fighting for control of my brain and body, and it felt like nobody was winning the argument.

I pulled forward, found second, and drove around the front of the building like I had every right to do so. Up the driveaway, checking the rear view mirror; no pursuit. At the main road, I realized I really didn't know where I was or how to get back to L.A. Okay, head downhill, I told myself. Eventually you'll hit 66 and turn right, or the Pacific Coast Highway and turn left, and then you'll see something you recognize.

Almost as soon as I hit the main road, the side of the canyon wall overshadowed me and I fumbled for the headlight switch. I had no idea how long it would be before Grayson knew I was gone, and I put my foot down. The road snapped back and forth, each twist throwing me alternately into waning sunlight or deep shadow. Every turn and every gear change tugged at my torn shoulder. As the road turned outward from the hill, I glanced up. I didn't see anything following me yet, but a pursuing car could easily be out of sight on the twists and turns. I was going into the curves too fast, braking too hard, and accelerating too harshly, and I was scaring myself.

As I rounded yet another tight turn with a one hundred foot drop to my right, I felt the back wheels start to slide. I felt terror rising in a flood. Instinctively, I came off the accelerator; the only thing I remembered from my driving lessons was not to brake. The car scrabbled terrifyingly for a moment, regained its grip and straightened, and I could steer again. I picked up the throttle again, a little more gently this time. Adrenaline was edging me over from brave to reckless; I needed to inject just a little caution if I was going to make it down in one piece.

I stopped looking back. It wouldn't help me. A car behind me could be anybody, I just had to assume Grayson or his people would be following, and the only thing I could do was keep heading downhill faster than them.

The climb was getting less steep now, the turns wider. I hoped it meant I was close to the bottom. Finally, I found a longer stretch that, while not exactly straight, curved only gently around an outcropping. About a hundred yards ahead, the road disappeared into fog and I thought I might finally be close to the ocean.

I hit the fog far too fast. The curve tightened without warning. I panicked and stamped the brakes hard and felt the backend fishtail. I tried to straighten it up but overcorrected. For a moment, it felt like the car was straightening out, then it twitched again and swung all the way around. Before I could do anything I was traveling backwards and knew I had to just ride it out. I braced myself against the steering wheel as the car rolled back into a wooden barrier that did nothing to slow it, off the road, down a bank, and into a thicket. The impact jolted every part of me and sent a wave of pain through my shoulder so intense it made me feel like throwing up. Bile rose, burning my throat, and I forced it back down.

The engine stalled.

I rested and breathed slowly for a minute or so, my heart pounding in my ears.

I didn't bother trying to restart the car; it wasn't going anywhere without the help of a tow truck. I pushed open the door, slid out and down onto the dirt, and scrambled my way up the slope back to the road. Scree scattered behind me, pinging loudly off the car; I felt like every step I took I slid half a step back. I was on hands and knees most of the way. At the top, I stood exhausted on the roadway. I realized I'd left my shoes behind. I wasn't going back for them; there was no possibility I could make the climb a second time.

I looked back at the car, lodged with one front wheel cocked in the air like a dog offering a handshake. It was scratched all over and dented everywhere I could see. The windshield was cracked, perhaps from one of the stones I had kicked backwards. Somebody was going to be filing an interesting insurance claim. I couldn't tell whether the car was visible from the road. Not that there was anything I could do about it.

I started walking down the road, wincing and hopping each time a pebble pierced my sole. The fog quickly cleared; the tight curve that had undone me evidently sat in a low fog hollow. About thirty feet ahead of me was a Stop sign, a highway, and beyond that the Pacific. I had hit the PCH. The air smelled of salt and rotting seaweed. Everything was lit in pale red by the last rays of the dying sunset. In my whole life I had never been so happy to see the ocean. I picked my way carefully down to the highway. To the north, the road wrapped around a headland and disappeared. To the south, about a hundred feet down, stood a gas station. I hoped they had a phone. Placing my steps cautiously on the stony roadside, I headed south. Every step was painful to my battered and tired body, even when I missed the stones.

The gas station was barely big enough to justify the name, just one pump and a wooden shack about six feet by eight, its planks stripped to gray by the salt air. A large window on the front was crusted with sand. Somebody had tried their best to wipe a couple of portholes so that the occupant of the shack could keep an eye out for customers.

I pushed open the door and surprised a boy of about seventeen who was bent over the counter reading a newspaper. He was tall and lanky and looked like he'd bend in a strong wind. His hair looked like he had combed it with water and his fingers. His hands were stained a patchy black from some mix of newsprint and oil. He raised his gaze from his newspaper and his face changed to an expression of shock. I realized how terrible I must look.

He stared for a few moments before speaking. "Ma'am, would you like to clean up?" he said. He offered me a key attached to a slab of wood bigger than my hand. "There's a bathroom around the back." I nodded and thanked him, took the key, and made my way around the shack. The bathroom was a smaller, faded clapboard shack with a tarpaper roof, assembled so randomly it might have been constructed from driftwood. I opened the padlock holding the door closed against the onshore breeze. Inside, it smelled of everything roadside bathrooms always do. The basin had only a cold tap. I was so grateful I momentarily considered adopting the boy.

I examine myself in the rust-pocked mirror. My face was bruised on both sides and I had dried blood on my cheek. There was a distinct scratch where Dolores had cut me. My hands were streaked with dirt and my fingernails a mess, too. The hand towel was barely less dirty than my hands, but I soaked it in water and dabbed myself clean as best I could. There was nothing I could do about the bruises. I stood there for a minute longer, trying to figure out what story to tell the boy. I could hardly believe the truth myself, and didn't expect him to, either. Finally I felt about as composed as I was going to get. I walked back around and returned the key to him.

"Ma'am, I don't mean to pry," he said, his voice close to breaking. "But did your husband do this?"

That seemed like a good story. I nodded. "I was trying to get away from him. I ran my car off the road about a hundred feet north of here, at the intersection."

"Is it okay to drive? Do you need a tow truck? It might take a couple of hours to get one out here."

"I don't think it's going anywhere by itself. Do you have a phone? I need to call for a taxi."

He pulled the phone out from a shelf under the counter and set it in front of me. "You're welcome to try," he said, "but you'll be lucky to get a cab to come all the way out here."

I asked the operator to connect me to Red Star's dispatch number. I'd had it memorized since the first time I saw it on the side of Joy's cab. For once, my weird memory for details was earning its keep. The line rang twice before it was picked up. I was lucky: Madge hadn't left yet.

"Madge?" I said. "It's Dot. I need a pickup, urgently."

"Where are you?" the grainy voice on the other end asked. I asked the boy. He told me the name of the road where I'd lost the car, and I relayed it to Madge.

"Okay," said the voice. "But it's going to take thirty or forty minutes for anybody to get out there. Are you safe where you are?" I assured her I was and hung up.

"Wow," said the boy. "You must have friends in the taxi business."

Yes, I thought, I must have. "It's going to be half an hour or more," I said. "Is it okay if I wait in here? I'll try to stay out of the way."

"Sure," said the boy. "And there's a chair out front if you want to sit." The chair wouldn't have fitted inside the tiny shack.

We were interrupted by the dinging of a bell.

"Customer. Excuse me," said the boy. I looked out the window and saw Grayson's black stretch De Soto. I scuttled behind the counter and ducked down, squeezed against the boy's legs.

"Is that your husband?" he asked anxiously.

"Yes!" I whispered.

"Don't worry," he said. "I'll take care of it." I hoped he didn't mean he was going to try to fight Grayson, especially not if he had one of his men with him. I waited an agonizing minute.

Finally, he returned. "He wanted to know if I'd seen a black Ford Deluxe come through. I told him I'd seen some traffic in both directions, but hadn't paid it enough attention to say what kinds of cars there were. He asked if there was a town near here and I told him to head north about a mile."

"Thank you so much!" I gasped. I realized I didn't even know this wonderful boy's name. We exchanged introductions; he was Thomas. I thanked him again.

It was getting dark now. Thomas turned on the naked yellow bulb that hung in the shack. I sat outside, watching the road and waiting for the taxi to arrive. I was safe for the moment, but it was only a matter of time before Grayson came after me again. I had to find a way to bring this whole business to an end.

Chapter Seventeen

It was Geoff who picked me up, and to my surprise Madge was sitting alongside him. Both of them stared openly at the state of me. I thanked Thomas profusely one final time and got in. Madge climbed in the back with me. She reached out to touch the bruises on my right cheek. I flinched and she thought better of it. I explained the events of the day as best I could, that the book that had been the cause of Mikey's beating was the reason for mine, too. She confirmed my fear: Joy was overdue to bring her cab back to the garage. For the remainder of the ride, I alternately brooded and dozed. My adrenaline rush was over, leaving me drained, exhausted, and bruised in too many places to count.

Geoff dropped us at Madge's apartment building. It was thoroughly dark by the time we got there, the street lamps casting a jaundiced yellow sheen over everything. She lived in a red brick building close to West Hollywood. "It's nothing special," said Madge. "But the Red Line runs right by here, which is handy."

Inside, the lobby was about as shabby as my own building. There was a porter's desk but no porter. There never was, Madge explained. It was a relic from a time when it had been a distinctly nicer neighborhood. The heavy wooden paneling on the doors, badly in need of repainting, and the dusty chandelier overhead, told the same story. We walked up to her second floor apartment. It bore all the same, distinctive hallmarks of bachelor living that my own apartment and Dalton's apartment shared. A dinner table big enough for two but set for one; a kitchenette just large enough to make coffee; a small sofa, an armchair, and a bare coffee table. So many people living alone in this city, I thought.

Madge showed me the bathroom, and I tried to clean myself up a little better. Meanwhile, she made coffee for both of us and poured a shot of whiskey in mine. We talked as we drank.

"What now?" asked Madge.

"I'm back where I started, only worse. I have to get the book back," I told her. "I can't let Grayson keep it, it's the only thing that will get Joy released by Accardo. And I have to do it soon. As long as Grayson has it, he's not going to let up."

"Do you know where it is?" she asked.

"I'm guessing Grayson has it stashed at his casino. He felt secure enough to hold me there, so it makes sense he would keep the book there, too. And he'll want it close by for when he gets his hands on me again. So I have to go back."

"Are you crazy?" exclaimed Madge. "You only just got out of there half-alive, and you're going to walk right back in?"

It did seem irrational, I had to admit. But I really didn't see any choice. In fact, my choices had been increasingly forced for days now. I stared off into the distance and let my brain wander. I called up details in my mind's eye, recalled everything I had seen in my two visits. After some minutes - I have no idea how many, but my coffee was not yet completely cold - I had at least an outline of a plan.

I realized Madge was staring at me.

"Where did you go?" she asked.

"My thinking place. Sorry. Is there a phone near here?"

"The restaurant on the corner has a payphone. We should probably get something to eat, anyway. And some rye for you before you drink all my whiskey."

It was a short walk to the restaurant at the end of the block. It was close to eight by now, and the place was quiet, the after-work rush long gone. A waitress brought us water and menus and I asked for a rye from the bar, a large one. Over the pork chop and mashed potatoes special, I told Madge my plan. She reaffirmed her opinion that I was crazy. She was probably right. The plan was completely insane, and yet still better than any alternative I could envision.

After dinner, I felt refreshed and ready for round two. I found the payphone and called Ginnie. Fortunately, she was home. I told her I didn't want to explain over the phone, and asked her to come over to Madge's apartment later.

"Can you drive yourself?" I asked. "I don't want to involve anybody else in this if we don't have to."

"Of course," she replied. "I'll bring the coupé."

"One more thing," I said. "What size shoe do you wear?"

By the time I got back to the table, Madge had already paid the check, which was handy since my purse, I realized, was still in my office where Grayson had snatched me hours before. She'd also bought a pint of rye to take back with us. I thanked her yet again.

Madge and I sat in her apartment with the radio playing show tunes and chatted. Or at least, she shared stories about the drivers while I listened and laughed as appropriate. Joy hadn't been kidding about the craziness of the midnight shift, and the celebrity names that came up shocked me. I was beginning to realize how carefully their public images were curated for our consumption. Much like Grayson presented himself as no more than a slightly shady businessman when in reality, he was a thug and possibly a killer.

There was a knock on the door around ten. Madge let Ginnie in. She was wearing another perfectly matched outfit, black linen slacks and a cobalt blue blouse. No jewelry, as I'd requested. She paused to wordlessly take in the state of my bruises before holding out two pairs of shoes to me.

"Heels or flats?" she asked. She offered a pair of scarlet open toes with a moderately sensible one inch heel and a pair of black patent leather pumps. I eyed the heels enviously but chose the sensible pumps. She must have seen my look.

"You can keep the heels, too," she said. "I won't wear them again."

I thanked her. It seemed like I had a lot of people to thank today.

With the three of us in the apartment, it felt almost crowded, Madge and I on the sofa and Ginnie in the one easy chair, but nobody seemed to mind, not even me. Madge shared her whiskey with Ginnie, and I sipped my rye. None of our glasses matched, and nobody seemed to mind that, either. I brought Ginnie up to date with the events of the day.

"So you think Accardo has snatched Joy, and you know Grayson wants to grab you, and the notebook is the solution to all your problems?" said Ginnie. She sounded skeptical.

"If it isn't, I don't know what is," I said. "I haven't got the whole thing worked out in my head, but the first step has to be to get my hands on the book." I was reminded of a conversation I'd had with Joy that felt like years ago but could only have been a little over a week. She had asked me if the plans I made in my head ever worked out; and I'd admitted no, they hardly ever did. This time, maybe it would be better not to have a plan.

I told Ginnie my intentions. I told her it was very dangerous. I reminded her that Joy and I were practically strangers and she didn't owe us this.

"I know, but I do owe it to John," she said. "And besides, this is by far the most exciting thing that has happened to me in years."

"You can just drive me there and wait outside if you want," I told her.

"No. I'm all in," she replied.

We talked and smoked until eleven thirty or so, pacing ourselves with the drinks. None of us could afford to be drunk for tonight's adventure, but I needed something for my nerves. My adrenaline rush had long since subsided. Ginnie said that the drive up to the casino would take around forty minutes at night. The place closed at midnight, and we should allow maybe an hour for the staff to clean up and leave, but it was just a guess. I told Madge not to wait up; I would stay the night with Ginnie. Of course, that assumed we got in and out of the casino as planned.

Ginnie and I walked out to her car, a gorgeous, two door Cadillac 62 Coupe in midnight blue with whitewall tires. She did everything with style, even breaking and entering.

"This is for when I'm driving myself," she said, sliding behind the wheel. "The only time the chauffeur gets to touch it is to wash it." The car drifted away from the curb like a boat slipping its moorings and purred up the street.

Neither of us spoke much on the way up. My anxiety was lower than I expected; perhaps I had burned out my capacity for anxiety for the day. Or perhaps it was simply acceptance of the inevitability of the path I was now on. We drove past the garage, barely visible in the dark, and turned right at the corner where I'd ditched the car. The wreck was invisible. I hoped the car's owner wasn't too upset. Ginnie drove uphill far more competently than either of my previous drivers and a lot more safely than I had driven down. As we came up on the last bend before the turnoff for the casino, she killed the headlights, causing me to gasp in surprise. There was just enough moonlight to see the edge of the road. We went past the entrance about a hundred feet and Ginnie turned around, headed back down about fifty feet, and pulled onto the shoulder.

Once our eyes had fully adjusted to the dark, we had a good view of the front the building and the car park. There were only a couple of cars remaining. She pulled a gold-plated cigarette holder out of her purse, offered me one and took one for herself, and lit them both. They looked much thinner than any cigarette I had seen, and tasted incredibly smooth. Hand rolled and a custom blend, I imagined. I suddenly realized how badly I needed a cigarette and I relished this one.

By the time we had finished, the car park was empty. We waited a few more minutes to be sure, and Ginnie took off the handbrake and let the car roll almost silently down the hill, before turning into the casino. The only sound was the crunch of gravel under our tires. We glided to a stop just past the valet station. The building was completely dark, the car park lit wanly by the moonlight and slashed by the shadows of the surrounding trees. We went around the side to the service door and I picked the lock in seconds.

"That was quick!" whispered Ginnie.

"It doesn't take long if you don't care about leaving marks," I whispered back. "And tonight, I don't care." We went inside, through the locker room and kitchen, into the restaurant, and out to the lobby. There was the door to the casino, which I glanced at ruefully, reminded of my ordeal earlier in its secret back room. Next to it was what I hoped was the door to Grayson's office. That lock also quickly succumbed to two bobby pins. Inside, I flicked on the flashlight I had borrowed from Madge. The office was as immaculate as one of Grayson's suits. Low wooden filing cabinets against one wall, a desk with its blotter, pen, and in-tray perfectly squared off; behind it a high-backed, leather chair; and behind that sat a three-shelf bookcase. In the light of the flashlight, everything looked a sickly yellow; I imagined in daylight it would all be perfectly matched in tastefully muted shades.

I went around the other side of the desk. There were two drawers. I opened the top one. It contained a check book, a receipt book, and an IOU book in duplicate, presumably for customers who gambled more than they could cover in cash. I closed it and opened the bottom one. There were several files of no interest, nothing else. Frustrating.

I stopped and thought.

Suddenly, it struck me. I pulled out the top drawer, turned it over, emptying it onto the floor, and placed it upside down on the desk. I turned and scanned the bookshelves, and on top found exactly what I needed: a stainless steel tchotchke about the size of a baseball, engraved with some curlicued writing. Some award for his business acumen or civic responsibility, no doubt. I hefted the award in my palm and smashed it down on the bottom of the drawer. It cracked. I hit it two more times and it splintered.

Picking the pieces apart and tossing them aside, I revealed the drawer's hidden compartment, and inside it the notebook. I felt very pleased with myself. Then I felt slightly foolish; there surely had to have been an easier way to open the compartment. Still, it felt like satisfying payback. I shoved the notebook into my skirt pocket where it bumped against the handcuffs. I'd forgotten I was still carrying those.

Suddenly, we heard the clop of footsteps on the lobby floor. We both startled and froze. I flicked off the flashlight. A voice came out of the darkness. It was Grayson's unmistakable faux-English accent. He must keep it up all the time, I thought.

"Who's there? Come out! I have a gun!" he shouted.

Ginnie put a finger to her lip, shushing me. "Anthony? It's me, Ginnie Townsend," she called out. She stepped out of the office and I could see the two of them silhouetted against the windows by the weak moonlight.

"Ginnie? What are you doing here? We're closed!"

He tucked his gun into his waistband.

"I'm sorry, I think I left my purse here tonight. I thought you might have put it in your office for safe keeping."

"How did you even get in?" he asked. "My office was locked, and so were the front doors." He sounded very skeptical.

Ginnie faked a tiny wobble. "Are you drunk?" he asked.

"Perhaps a little," said Ginnie, and stumbled theatrically to one side.

Grayson reached out and grabbed her by the elbows and set her upright. "Wait a minute," he said. "Were you even here tonight?"

And that was when I hit him behind the ear with his award for Restaurateur of the Year, 1944. He went down in comically slow motion and folded himself into a pile.

I prodded him with the toe of Ginnie's borrowed shoe. "Should I hit him again?" I asked.

"I don't think that's necessary," replied Ginnie.

"Oh, Mr. Grayson and I are well beyond 'necessary'," I said. I took his gun. If he were to follow us, I didn't want him armed. I did leave him his award, though.

We went back out the way we'd come in, slid into the car, drove downhill. Neither of us spoke.

After ten tense minutes she broke the silence. "Dammit!"

"What?" I asked, alarmed.

"I'm going to have find a new place to play roulette."

Halfway down the hill, I tossed Grayson's gun over the side of the canyon. I didn't know how to use it and I didn't want to. I'd seen enough guns in the past two weeks and none of them had meant anything good.

Ginnie drove us back to her house and let us in through the door from the motor court. The place was dark and she fumbled for a light switch.

The creases between my eyebrows showed my anxiety. "I can't stay here tonight. Grayson saw you. He'll figure it out. I should go back to Madge's apartment."

"It'll be fine," Ginnie said. "He won't come here. Too many of his customers are friends of mine, and so is the D.A. out in San Bernadino. I could do a lot of damage to his business if he crossed me, and he knows it. You'll be out of harm's way, and the book can go in my safe. "

I felt the beginnings of reassurance. "I don't have anything to wear, though."

"I have pajamas you can borrow, and I'm sure one of the bedrooms must be made up," she told me. "And tomorrow I'll lend you some clean clothes."

"Okay, but on one condition. When I get up tomorrow, I want to change into lounging pajamas!"

Ginnie laughed. "I'm sure that can be arranged."

She quickly found pajamas for me and a room close to hers. Neither one of us was ready for bed, though; we were both still too ramped up from the night's adventures. We retired - that was Ginnie's word - to the front salon, and Ginnie brought out the Scotch and two cut crystal glasses. We sipped slowly while we replayed the evening's events to each other, coloring the narrative with our competing degrees of excitement and fear.

I told her how much I admired her little improvisation with Grayson, and she returned the compliment regarding my blow to his head. A little something I learned from watching Joy, I told her, and shared the unredacted story of our visit to Dalton's apartment.

I reflected that I desperately needed to keep friends like Joy and Ginnie in my life.

It was sometime in the small hours of Saturday morning when we both finally felt sufficiently wound down for bed.

"I'll have Simmons wake you with coffee at ten, if that's alright. He's used to me rising late."

I slept in silk pajamas between satin sheets and dreamed of beautiful motor cars.

The next morning, Simmons woke me as promised. After coffee, I dressed in a pair of Ginnie's lounging pajamas that Simmons had laid out for me and went in search of her. I found her in the front parlor again, drinking tea. I asked for coffee and she sent the unhappy Simmons off to find some.

"What will you do now?" Ginnie asked once I was settled.

"I don't know. Before, it seemed like the best thing to do was to give the book to Grayson or Accardo and get them off my back; presumably, Accardo, once he took Joy," I responded. "But after Grayson snatched me, I realized not even that helps. Either one of them will still want me to decode the book, which will get a lot of people blackmailed again. And it's pretty likely that some of them are like you and don't deserve it."

"And whichever one of them you don't give it to is going to be mad at you," said Ginnie.

"Yes, thank you for reminding me of that."

I finished my coffee, and Ginnie set me up with a pair of cream cotton slacks, a bright red pullover, and a pair of black ballerina flats. The slacks were very handy, given I'd completely wrecked another pair of stockings in my escape from Grayson's casino. I slipped the handcuffs into the pocket. Ginnie fetched the notebook from the safe and I took it back to the parlor where I sat and stared at it while my coffee went cold. An hour later, I still hadn't found any crack to open the code up. I had been hoping some repeated word like "politician" or "actor" might break me in, but there was nothing I could see. No wonder Dalton had been frustrated by it.

I was interrupted by Ginnie calling to me from the hall. "Madge is on the phone for you. Can you pick up the extension?"

I looked around and noticed an extension phone sitting on the sideboard in front of the fake tapestry. I picked it up and heard Ginnie hang up the other phone.

"Some guy named Accardo called and said to meet him at your shop in an hour," Madge said.

"But Grayson is looking for me. Surely he'll have the shop watched?" I objected.

"Accardo said not to worry about Grayson. He has been, to use his words, warned off."

I sighed heavily. Meeting Accardo again was so obviously a bad idea, but as long as he held Joy, I didn't see what else I could do. Ginnie put the notebook back in her safe to alleviate my anxiety about Grayson.

Ginnie offered me the use of Toby and the Lincoln, which I gratefully accepted, not least because it would be by far the most beautiful car I had ever ridden in. I reclined in the back seat for the ride over to the store. The leather seats were softer than my bedsheets. Money might not buy happiness, but it certainly bought nice automobiles. I tried not to stare too much at Toby's perfect profile.

Inside the store, I retrieved my purse, which had been sitting in my office since Grayson abducted me, and stashed the handcuffs in it. I didn't know why I was keeping them, but they seemed like an appropriate souvenir.

All I could do was wait for Accardo. I turned the sign in the window to Closed; I didn't want to have customers in the store when Accardo showed up.

Around noon, Accardo's chauffeur pulled up in the red Caddy and they performed the same ritual with the coat and hat. Accardo came in and latched the door behind him. I walked out to meet him in the middle of the room but he kept coming forward, pushing me back until I bumped into my desk. He stood uncomfortably close, forcing me to look up at him. If his business was menacing people, I had to concede he was very good at it.

He reached out and grasped my chin between his forefinger and thumb. I tried to resist, but he forced my head first to the left and then to the right, examining my bruises with what I took to be professional interest.

"Grayson is such an amateur!" he said, making no attempt to hide his disgust.

"He seemed to be pretty good at this," I said, gesturing at the purple and blue mosaics on my cheeks.

"And what did it get him?"

"Nothing, I guess."

"Do you have my book?" he demanded.

"Not with me," I replied. "It's secure. Somewhere I can retrieve it when I need it, but not immediately." It was close enough to the truth.

"You need it tonight," said Accardo. "I'm done waiting. So far, Joy is unharmed, and I'm sure you want to it to stay that way. Once you've given me the book and the key to decode it, our business will be concluded."

"And the thousand dollars?" I asked. I wasn't optimistic.

"Last week's offer is not this week's offer," he replied. And with that, he turned and left.

I sat down in my office chair and waited for my breathing and heartbeat to return to normal. Afterward, I opened my own notebook, turned to a blank page, and started writing down everything I knew about my situation, what Grayson wanted, what Accardo wanted, and what they were willing to do. I sketched pictures and I drew lines connecting things and I scribbled and I crossed things out and wrote them again. I didn't like any of my conclusions.

I took a cab back to Ginnie's place, an indulgence I couldn't afford but definitely needed. For a couple of hours, I played with the code some more but made no more progress than I had the first time.

By three o'clock, I knew what I had to do. I picked up the phone. My first call was to Madge. I outlined the plan to her. She was enthusiastic and promised to arrange everything as I had described. Next, I called Grayson. A girl answered the phone and I told her who I was. She asked me to hold. A minute went by before I heard an extension pick up and Grayson's voice come on.

"What do you want, witch?" he snarled.

At least, I told myself that was what he called me. It wasn't a very clear line. "I've decided to put an end to this," I replied. "Meet me at the Red Star taxi garage at one in the morning and you can have the book."

"And the code?"

"I've broken it. You can have the key, too. I just want this to be over."

"Very well," he said. "If you deliver as promised, I don't see any more reason to bother you."

"Good. Come alone. And one more thing: no guns. I'm tired of having guns pointed at me. If I see a gun, the notebook disappears. Understood?"

There was a pause, I presumed while Grayson thought about interesting ways to break the agreement. "Agreed," he replied, and hung up.

I listened to the dead line for a few seconds before hanging up myself. I took a few deliberate breaths to steady myself and fished in my purse for the card Accardo had left me on his first visit to my store. I dialed his number. This time, it was a male voice who answered, not one I recognized.

"Tell Accardo that Stone is calling." I heard a muffled relay of my message, then footsteps, then Accardo.

"Well?"

"First, I need to know that Joy is okay. Put her on, please." There was a long pause with some shuffling noises. My anxiety was tying knots in my neck muscles as I waited for her to come on the line.

"Hey, kid. How are you doing?"

I exhaled the breath I hadn't even realized I'd been holding. "Fine," I replied. "More importantly, how are you?"

"Well, they keep me tied to a chair and a guy stands outside when I go to the bathroom, but other than that, they've been perfect gentlemen."

Accardo's voice came back on. "Okay, that's enough. Satisfied?"

"Yes, thank you. I'm prepared to give you the book and the key in return for Joy's safe release. You said tonight. Can you bring her to the Red Star garage at one in the morning?"

"Why so late?" he asked.

"Because there won't be anybody coming and going at that hour. The shift changeover is at midnight."

"Okay, that's alright."

"Bring Moretti, too. I have words for him. And no guns or the whole thing is off. I hate the sight of guns."

"Yeah, sure," said Accardo. "Is that everything?"

"Yes," I said.

He hung up.

My heart was pounding. I opened up Hooke's notebook again, the Vanity Fair on the side table. Regardless of circumstances, focusing on a code was guaranteed to center me, bring me back to calm. And even though I couldn't crack this one, I was beginning to suspect I knew why. Another hour and I was confident I knew.

"Clever boy, Hooke," I said out loud. I promised myself I would drink a respectful shot to his ghost later.

Ginnie and I had dinner together. I didn't tell her my intentions; only that I would be out that night. I didn't want her volunteering to get involved. She'd already risked more than enough for me, and what I had planned for later could go badly wrong. I did let her lend me Toby again, and he took me over to Jack's bar where I was hoping to find a few of the drivers to keep me company.

I wasn't disappointed. Madge was at a table with a dozen drivers, most of whom I recognized. Once this was over, I really needed to make more effort to remember their names,

I told myself. Names were the one thing that did not come easily to my oddly specific memory.

I joined them and listened to the chatter. Mikey had been discharged from the hospital and one of the drivers had taken him home. He was still sore and his hearing in one ear hadn't returned yet, but the doctors promised it would. The other drivers had set up a rota to check up on him for the next couple of days, just to be sure. After that, he would be working in the garage again, but no driving until at least the end of another week. I felt relieved. Nobody brought up Joy's abduction, which made me think Madge had kept it to herself. I was grateful.

Other drivers came and went, the ones with families leaving by seven and the number slowly dwindling after that. By eight, it was just Madge and me. We were drinking mostly water, but Jack didn't seem to mind. It was going to be another long night.

"We could go to my apartment and you could get a couple of hours' sleep," suggested Madge.

"Thanks, but I'm too keyed up. I've promised myself I'll sleep for twenty-four hours when this is over, though," I replied. "You can go home, really. You don't need to stay around for this."

"What will you do?" she asked.

"I'll stay here and see if that's really true," I said, pointing to the sign in the window that said, 'We never close'.

Madge laughed. "I've wondered that myself. I'll keep you company for a little while yet."

A few minutes before eleven, she excused herself, explaining she had to catch the last streetcar home. I thanked her again for everything she'd done for me. She wished me luck. If everything went the way I had rehearsed it in my head, I wouldn't need it. And if it didn't, luck wouldn't help.

I went over and sat up at the bar, watching Jack cleaning glasses and gently letting the late night drunks know they were cut off. He kept me supplied with water and tall tales of previous customers, and around midnight, I had one more rye to steady my nerves. We were the last two in the place. That was another first for me.

Chapter Eighteen

I arrived at the garage around fifteen minutes before one. I needed to be there ahead of Grayson and Accardo. As I descended the ramp, my footsteps reverberated back and forth until three, four, five steps sounded one on top of the other. I went into Madge's dispatch box and turned on the lights down the center of the ceiling, leaving the sides of the garage in darkness. Stepping out of the box, my shadow stretched out along the ground behind me and disappeared into the dark. Along each side of the garage, ten taxis were parked facing each other. The rest of the cabs were out working the midnight shift. They wouldn't be back for hours.

I picked up the flashlight Madge had left in her booth and made a quick circuit of the garage to ensure there were no surprises. Now I had to wait. The garage was silent apart from the buzz of fluorescent lights overhead and water dripping slowly somewhere at the back.

A couple of minutes after one, I heard a car pull up. The engine burbled for a moment and died. Two doors slammed, one close after the other, then a pause and a third slammed. Accardo, Moretti, Joy. My pulse pounded in my head and I could feel adrenaline rising. I forced myself to take several deep, slow breaths to try to settle myself. It might have helped, but not much.

I waited impatiently as they entered the ramp and made their way down, stepping around the pools of oil and water, the two mobsters each holding one of Joy's arms. At first, their shadows trailed them all the back way to the entrance, then shortened as they got close to the nearest light and turned into a small puddle as they passed underneath it. They came to a stop under one of the lights, facing me, about ten feet away. Joy was dwarfed between the two stocky men, each with a hand the size of a baseball mitt on her shoulder.

"Joy, everything alright?" I called out. My voice echoed between the walls, the ceiling, the floor, slowly dying away. Listening to myself, I sounded a lot more calm than I was feeling.

"Yeah," she replied. "Accardo has been very professional about everything." I noticed she didn't say anything about Moretti.

"Okay, gentlemen, open your jackets, please," I said to the two men. "I want to see you don't have guns."

They did as I asked. Accardo smirked; he clearly believed he didn't need a gun tonight. "Can we get started now?" he said truculently.

"Not just yet. We're still waiting for one thing," I replied. I heard another car pull up; I listened to its engine idle and shudder to a stop. The door slammed. "And that's it."

Moretti and Accardo turned to the entrance and saw Grayson coming down the ramp.

"What the hell?" said Accardo.

Grayson stopped, looked behind him as if he were considering bailing out, then continued. He came to the center of the garage and stood a couple of feet away from Accardo and out of reach of Moretti. Sensible choice, I thought. "What the hell is this?" asked Grayson, gesturing at the others.

He looked angry. Accardo and Moretti didn't look happy, either.

Good. I was done with pleasing them. "I decided it would be simplest to get everybody together and sort this thing out once and for all," I said. "Now, open your jacket and show me you don't have a gun. Otherwise, Moretti will probably hit you and take it away."

Moretti grinned. I figured he didn't need much excuse to hit people. Grayson peered around Accardo at Moretti and opened his jacket.

"Thank you. This is all going to be very civilized, I hope, and everybody will leave happy."

"Or I could just have Moretti knock everybody about a bit and take the notebook," said Accardo. Moretti grinned again.

"Obviously, I don't have the book here. I'm not naive. Any violence, and you never see it, guaranteed. First Joy goes free, then I explain my other terms. Then and only then, I fetch the book."

Grayson and Accardo glared at me. Moretti looked like he didn't care as long as he got to beat somebody up before the night was over.

"Cross me on this and I will make you regret it immediately," said Accardo.

"Fully understood," I replied.

Accardo took his hand from Joy's shoulder and nodded at Moretti to do the same. Joy shrugged some life back into her shoulders and walked across to me. That made me happy in more ways than one. I was counting entirely now on Accardo treating this as a business transaction, not a personal matter. As long as I avoided taunting or humiliating him, I felt confident it would stay that way, and Joy's release was a good sign. Grayson was less predictable, but I hoped the presence of Accardo and Moretti would keep him in line.

"You can go home now, Joy," I said. "I'll handle the rest."

"No way," she replied. "I'm sticking with you to the end."

I could see there was no point arguing with her. "Okay," I said. "There's been a change of plans. I've decided to keep the book. It's going to keep me and my friends safe." This was a very dangerous moment. Everything hinged on what happened next, on Accardo and Grayson hearing me out.

Grayson was the first to react. "What?" he said. "You lied to me!"

"Yes," I replied. "But it was endearing of you to believe me."

He scowled.

"Do we have to do this all over again?" asked Accardo. He was simmering, but under control. "I can take the girl again any time I want, and next time, I won't be so polite." Moretti was just waiting for a signal to be let off the leash.

"No," I said to Accardo. "It's over. And here's why. I broke the code. I know all the dirty secrets of your political friends. Hooke had a real talent for acquiring dirt. And Grayson suggested to me that it would be hugely damaging to your business if they were exposed and had to leave their positions."

Accardo looked furious. He grabbed Grayson by the arm, and Grayson jerked himself free. I heard his sleeve tear. That would annoy him, I thought happily.

"Give me the damn book or I will kill you both!" yelled Accardo.

"That won't help you either, I'm afraid," I said. "I've made copies of the relevant pages and mailed them to friends. They have instructions to keep mailing them to each other, so they'll permanently be circulating in the mail system. If anything happens to me or my friends, they go to the D.A. By the way, that was Grayson's idea, too." The last was a lie, but I enjoyed telling it.

"Wait, what?" said Grayson, his face contorted in alarm.

Accardo grabbed for him again, and he lurched out of reach.

"All you have to do is stay away from myself and my friends, and nothing will come out. Other than that, I don't care what you do, you and your corrupt friends," I said. "It's a dirty town, and nothing I can do will change that. I will stay out of your business and you will stay out of mine. That's my offer."

Accardo glared at me for a long time, slowly calming himself. I was still worried, but I hoped he was doing the mental calculus. Rationally, this was airtight. He liked to think of himself as a businessman, and he had to know this was the best deal he was getting. It kept him in business and in good standing with his bosses back in Chicago. And it was the only way this worked for me, too; I couldn't leave him with nothing to lose. Exposing his friends only helped me as long as it was a threat held in reserve. It all depended on him seeing it the same way and acting sensibly. Under the circumstances, there was no guarantee.

I waited. A car cruised along the street above the ramp, briefly casting jaundiced yellow light across half the garage.

"If you expose me, I will destroy you and your friend," he finally said. The calmness with which he delivered this was more frightening than anger.

"I understand. That's how this works."

"Agreed, then."

I turned to Grayson. "As for you, it's more personal." I touched a hand to the bruises on my right cheek. "You should know that I nurse grudges the way other women nurse babies. And your page in the notebook made for very interesting reading. I'm pretty sure you wouldn't want it to come out. So you, too, will stay away from me and everybody I know."

Grayson suddenly looked very pale.

"Is that it?" asked Accardo. I'd never seen a man contain so much anger yet project such calm. In a bizarre way, I actually admired his professionalism.

"One last thing. There has to be a reckoning. For Dalton. And for Mikey. Which one of you really killed Dalton?"

"I did," said Moretti without hesitation. "I enjoyed it, too. The punk wasn't giving up nothing, and he had a smart mouth. Don't even think about the body, it's gone."

I sighed. I wasn't in any way surprised, but it was still upsetting. "Thank you," I said, and raised my flashlight to the ceiling. That was the signal for twenty cabs to open their doors and for thirty or more cabbies to spill out. The doors slammed shut in a staccato cascade whose echoes slowly faded away. I looked around at the weapons they were carrying. I saw tire irons and hammers and wrenches, blackjacks and baseball bats, and a couple of sets of brass knuckles. No guns nor knives, as I'd requested. The drivers formed up in two lines facing each other. Their shadows loomed monstrously across the floor and up the walls like a child's worst nightmare.

Grayson, Accardo, and even Moretti looked around in alarm; all traces of anger were chased from their faces and replaced by the first awakenings of fear. The drivers on the ends of each line advanced a handful of steps, closing the ring around the three of them.

"I want Moretti," I said. "I want to turn him over to the police. He has to pay for Mikey, and they need somebody for the Boyle killing. Who knows, they might be able to fit him in the frame for Dalton, too, even without a body. And I don't think they'll care what condition he's in when we turn him over."

"Why would I ever agree to that?" growled Accardo.

"Because we both need them to close the file on Boyle's murder. If they keep poking at it, it's going to eventually lead them to me. And who knows what I might do with the notebook if that happened."

Accardo looked around again, assessing the situation and considering his options. I was so anxious, I was struggling to draw full breaths. My ribs felt like they might crush my heart.

"What the hell," he finally said. "Sure. You can have Moretti. He's too much of a loose cannon, anyway. Two dead, one in the hospital, and he still didn't get the book. I can't run a business that way. It's just unprofessional."

"What?" yelled Moretti, and with speed unexpected from such a big man, drew his arm back and punched Accardo in the side of the head. Accardo staggered three steps sideways, went down on one knee, got up again, wobbled for a moment, and went down once more.

"You two can go now," I said.

Accardo picked himself up again and weaved as best he could up the ramp, the ring of drivers opening briefly to let him pass through. He didn't look back. Grayson had watched the whole thing in horror, but now he unfroze and ran after Accardo, his elongated shadow spilling ahead of him.

The ring of drivers began closing in on Moretti, everybody cautious. They had heard what he had done to Mikey and seen what he had done to Accardo, and even in numbers, nobody wanted to get close to his fists. Suddenly, Moretti dipped down and grabbed for his right sock. His hand came up holding a small pistol that was almost entirely swallowed by his fist. And just as quickly, a tire iron came down and smacked into his wrist. He cursed profusely and grabbed his broken right wrist in his left hand, the gun clattering to the floor. Another tire iron crashed into his knee and he went down screaming. The rest of the drivers piled on.

I turned to Joy. "I don't need to watch this. I'm leaving. Are you coming?"

"Nah," she replied. "I want a piece of this." She tapped one of the other drivers on the arm. He pulled a blackjack from his pocket and handed it to her.

"Okay," I said. "Oh, you might need these when you're done," and I pulled the handcuffs from my pocket and handed them to Joy.

She waded into the crowd.

I turned and walked away. Up the ramp, right turn, and down the boulevard. As I walked, Moretti's cries grew fainter.

Past the park, then another right. I couldn't hear him at all now. It would take me forty minutes to walk home, and by the time I got there, maybe I'd be able to sleep.

I slept for ten hours, got up, used the bathroom, drank some water, and slept for eight more. It wasn't the twenty four hours of straight sleep I'd promised myself, but it would do.

Chapter Nineteen

Thursday afternoon found me at the Marmont hotel. Ginnie had called me at the store the previous day and proposed that she, I and Joy meet for cocktails. I hadn't seen her since the showdown with Grayson and Accardo, and I gratefully accepted. She had sent Toby over with a selection of clothes and shoes that she swore were too hopelessly unfashionable for her ever to wear again, but she assured me would be good enough for the tea room at the Marmont. I'd picked out a pair of cream linen pants with a three-button waistband that were artfully designed to make one's legs look longer, a crimson cotton blouse that was a very bold color for me, and a cravat of my own.

I was learning to like pants, especially since they meant I didn't have to worry about the state of my stockings. On my feet were the same ballerina flats she'd given me before our raid on Grayson's casino; they were my new favorite shoes. I had my raincoat folded over my arm because, of course, it was going to rain later. My bruises had mostly faded, and what remained I covered with foundation makeup. I felt like I could just about pass for the kind of socialite who drank afternoon cocktails at the Marmont.

I arrived at the lounge five minutes early and was surprised to see Joy was there before me. She was dressed much as she had been the first time I'd met her: khaki-colored gabardine slacks, a simple white blouse. She was also wearing the leather flight jacket, but now it was simply a reminder of happy times, not a memento mori.

"I got here early," she said. "I wanted to see whether they would let me in, dressed like this."

"Apparently not," I replied.

"They said they couldn't seat us until our whole party was here, which I think was code for 'We don't remotely believe you're being hosted by Ginnie Townsend'."

Ginnie chose that moment to make her entrance. She was as impressive as ever in a black wool dress that ended just above the knee, cut on the bias to hug her figure and follow her every move, and cinched at the waist by a wide, shiny black belt with a gold buckle. On her feet were patent leather heels with an open toe. She wore diamond studs in her ears and a matching pendant on a silver chain. It was simple yet perfect. I knew I would never wear her clothes the way she wore her clothes.

On seeing her approach, the hostess leapt to attention and came over. "How nice to see you Miss Townsend, and your companions!" She waved over a waitress and told her to check our coats for us. The waitress took my raincoat over one arm, and with the other hand held the collar of Joy's jacket between thumb and forefinger as if it might be contagious. Joy giggled.

A few minutes later, we were settled at our table, ordering the first of what I anticipated would be several rounds of drinks. I opted for a Manhattan, not least because it reminded me of Mikey, who was still on the mend but improving every day. Ginnie asked for a Rob Roy, which she told me was basically a Manhattan with Scotch instead of Rye. I looked at Joy.

"Sorry, Joy," I said teasingly. "This isn't exactly a beer and sawdust kind of place."

"I drank with airmen," she replied. "I can drink shots." She asked for a bourbon on the rocks.

When the drinks arrived, we made a simple toast to ourselves. I still couldn't quite believe I had known these two people for less than three weeks. It had certainly been the most frightening, confusing, and exhilarating three weeks of my life.

We sat in silence for a moment or two. Ginnie proposed a toast to me.

"Why?" I asked, embarrassed.

"Because of your remarkable skill. You managed to crack the code in one day. John had struggled for weeks and gotten nowhere. Without that, I hate to think how this would have played out."

"Ginnie's right," said Joy. "You put all the pieces together. You solved the puzzle."

We clinked our glasses and drank again. "Actually, I have a confession."

The other two looked at me expectantly.

"I couldn't break the code. Nobody could."

"But in the garage you said--" began Joy.

"All a bluff," I interrupted her.

They both looked stunned.

"But why is it so unbreakable?" asked Ginnie.

"Have either of you ever heard of a book cipher?" I asked.

Ginnie shook her head. Joy gave a short laugh.

"Sherlock Holmes. The Valley of Fear," she said. "Holmes gets a coded message in the mail, quickly figures out what the book is, and decodes it immediately."

"I'm still in the dark," said Ginnie.

"Go ahead," I told Joy. She was obviously bursting to explain it.

"The short version is that it's a way of coding a message using a book as the key," she said. "So say the first word I want to encode is 'money', I find the word 'money' in the book. And then I write down something that identifies the location of the word. For Holmes, it was page, column, and word number from an almanac."

"And you can use any book?" asked Ginnie.

"As long as it has the vocabulary you need," I said. "What makes it so hard to crack for somebody who doesn't have the book is that the person coding can use a different instance of the word each time".

"So what?"

"Usually to get started into a code, there's a lot of clues we can look for. We can look for sequences that come up frequently and guess it's a common word like 'the' or 'and'. And if we know what the message might be about, like military transmissions, we can guess at commonly-used words and try to find them in the code. But with a book cipher, every time a particular word appears, it might be coded differently because you can find it in lots of places in your book. The word 'and' might appear hundreds of times in the book, so each time you need to code it you can pick a different instance. That's why neither Dalton nor I could find any patterns. And that same lack of patterns is what made me suspect it's a book cipher. To have any real chance at a book cipher, somebody has to have the same book that was used to code the message in the first place. And not just the same book, but the exact same edition so that the pages and lines match up."

"An 1865 Vanity Fair, first American edition, for instance," said Joy.

"For instance," I echoed.

"Dalton thought the book mattered, maybe he figured it out too," murmured Ginnie thoughtfully. "But now you know what book you need…".

I shook my head. "I tried it already. I tried a bunch of typical encodings. Chapter number, line number, word number. Page, line, word number. A whole bunch of other schemes too. No dice."

"What does that mean?" asked Ginnie.

"I think it means he used something really clever, different from any of the usual schemes. It could be something trivial like just adding one to every number. Or it could be something insanely complicated. Even with the right edition of the right book in hand, you would spend a lifetime trying to figure it out. No, the secrets in that notebook died with Hooke."

We were all quiet for a moment and sipped our drinks.

"Poor John," said Ginnie. "We should drink to his memory, too. He wasn't a perfect man by any means, but he was a good one, and he didn't deserve to die over this."

We raised our glasses again. I thought about John Dalton, I man I had met only once and briefly, and yet knew better than either Joy or Ginnie did. I hoped it didn't show on my face.

Ginnie ordered another round for us.

"There's still a couple of things I don't understand," I said. "Grayson seemed very confident I could decode the book. How could he know that?"

"I have an idea about that," said Ginnie. "When I got up on Monday, Simmons was gone, his room cleared out."

"Meaning what?" asked Joy.

"Meaning I think he'd been listening in on my visitors and phone calls, and selling gossip about me to the columnists. And to Grayson, too. Society rumor has it that Grayson bought and sold dirt on everybody, especially his casino customers. And I think Simmons realized he'd given himself away."

"I thought staff were supposed to be more loyal than that," I said.

"Perhaps Simmons decided he was going to be out of a job once I sold the house, and decided to cash in while he still could," said Ginnie.

"Or maybe he was just a horrible person with an impressive English accent," I replied.

"Now what?" said Joy.

"What do you mean?" I asked.

"This has been a wild ride, but it's over now and I'm back where I was before," she said. "Just waiting for the day I go to the garage only to be told I don't have a drive because a vet needs a job. It's just a matter of time."

"That's got to be frustrating," I replied. "I suppose I still have the bookshop to go back to, although I can't say I'm excited by the prospect. And even that depends on finding a way to make more money. I'll probably make rent this month, but who knows about next month, or the month after."

"I have a suggestion," said Ginnie. We both looked at her hopefully.

"You've both proven yourself pretty damn good as investigators. Why don't you try making a business of it?"

Joy and I looked at each other. It sounded completely crazy.

"I can think of a ton of reasons why not, but number one would be money," I said. "There must be training, licenses, renting an office... all kinds of expenses. Plus, the time it takes to build up a reputation and a clientele. All money I don't have."

"I'm barely making a living as it is," said Joy. "If I start taking time off for something like that, they'll definitely give my drive away."

"I'll back you financially," said Ginnie.

"What?" I said. "I mean, that's incredibly generous, but that's way beyond giving me some of your old clothes. We couldn't possibly."

"Yes, you could," said Ginnie. "I have lots of money, and most of it just sits around making more money. Being your patron would be fun for me, too."

Joy and I looked at each other. I could tell we were both thinking about it.

"'Stone and D'Amico, Private Investigators,'" I said. "It does sound good, actually."

"'D'Amico and Stone' sounds better," replied Joy, smiling.

"Let's flip a coin for it," I said.

"That deserves another toast," said Ginnie. We raised our glasses again.

That evening, I sat at home alone with a half pint bottle of rye in front of me. I poured a glass for myself and another for John Dalton.

Joy was right. I had solved the puzzle. Just not the one I'd set out to solve. When I put the pieces together, only one picture made sense. Dalton had killed Hooke.

I had been full of questions about Dalton from the beginning. How did he get hold of the notebook? He couldn't have just picked it up. Hooke wouldn't leave something that valuable to himself lying around. It would either be on his person or safely locked away. So how did Dalton get to it before the police did?

And once he had the book, why was he so determined to decode it? Why didn't he destroy it, especially with Ginnie's name in there? Why would he not give it up, to the point it cost him his life? And why was there no case file for Hooke in Dalton's office?

And so I was forced to one conclusion. John Dalton had killed Hooke, and taken the notebook off of Hooke's dead body. Dalton had killed him because he found out he was blackmailing Ginnie. Whether he intended to kill Hooke, or just scare him off and it went horribly wrong, nobody would ever know. There was no case file because there was never a case; just Dalton and Hooke.

And once he had his hands on the notebook, Dalton saw a chance to solve his money problems. He wasn't trying to decode it out of some altruistic desire to identify the victims and let them know they were safe. Instead, he wanted the business for himself. If he couldn't make a living as an honest private eye, he would try making a living as a dishonest one.

Unfortunately for Dalton, other people wanted the business more. Dalton wasn't a good man, but I couldn't entirely condemn him as a bad man, either. He was just a desperate man who had played the cards he'd been dealt, and played them badly.

And I would never burden Joy or Ginnie with this. It was mine alone to carry. Let them have their memories of Dalton. I drank my rye and poured Dalton's down the sink.

Epilogue

Four months passed. Joy and I took classes and studied and passed the exams and got our private detective licenses. Joy got a firearms permit; I refused to touch a gun. Ginnie financed the remodeling of my store into our offices and promised to keep us afloat while we built up the business. She also leaned on a District Attorney whose re-election campaign needed her generosity and got us Special Deputy badges. They didn't mean much in reality, but they might open a few doors.

Finally, one day in the summer of 1946, we were ready. Ginnie, Joy, and I looked on as the former bookshop's new door went in. Sturdy hardwood, two locks, a single pane of frosted glass for privacy with bars behind for security. The sign painter was finishing up the gold lettering on the shop window:

D'Amico & Stone
Private Investigations

ABOUT THE AUTHOR

J.T. Berry has carefully avoided the kinds of jobs and adventures that make authors sound interesting in these biographies, apart perhaps from that one time in Czechoslovakia. After a first career that involved lots of office cubicles and slide presentations, J.T. is now attempting to make a living as a writer.